MW01697465

The Five Pillars Of Relationship Equity

The Practice of Fairness in a Romantic Relationship Using the Power of Two

DR. FEMI OGUNJINMI (GFEM), PH.D.

Founder of National Relationship Equity Day

THE FIVE PILLARS OF RELATIONSHIP EQUITY: The Practice of Fairness in a Romantic Relationship Using the Power of Two.

ISBN: 978-978-60038-7-0

Scriptures quotations marked, unless otherwise indicated, are taken from the Holy Bible, the New International Version, and the New King James Version NKJV of the Holy Bible.

Dr. Femi Ogunjinmi's book titles may be purchased in bulk for Educational, Ministerial, Business, Fundraising, or Sales Promotional use. For information, please email: Info@nationalrelationshipequityday.org

Mobile: +1 (443) 824-4182

Printed in the United States of America

Desingened & Published by

YPN Publishing & Media ®

Leading International Publishing and Media Group

Whatsapp +2348023768604

admin@ypnpublishers-media.com

www.ypnpublishers-media.com

@ypnpublishers

@ypnpublishingmedia

Table Of Contents

Dedication

I humbly dedicate this project to the divine presence of God and my cherished family, whose unwavering support and love have been instrumental in its fruition. Throughout the journey of creating this book, I have felt the guidance and grace of the Almighty, providing sustenance and divine encounters that have shaped its essence. My profound gratitude extends to my beloved best friend and wife, Victoria, affectionately known as My All-Inclusive Wife, for being a beacon of unwavering support and love during the challenging writing and research process. Your sacrifices, alongside those of our incredible children, Anu-Gabriella and Iyanu-Daniel, have been a constant source of inspiration, fueling my determination to reach new heights.

To my esteemed parents, Elder and Mrs. Claudius Ogunjinmi, your nurturing and the values you instilled in me have shaped the man I am today. Your strength, hard work, and resilience serve as an enduring example. I am forever grateful for the investment you made in my upbringing. Expressing heartfelt appreciation, I thank my parents-in-law, Pastor and Mrs. Makinde, for their persistent prayers, steadfast support, and boundless love. Your generous and nurturing spirits have embraced me as your own, and I am truly blessed to have you as part of my life.

Foreword

Dr. Ogunjinmi is widely regarded as the original philosopher and architect of the relationship equity concept. In addition to that, the Global Civility Leader 2020 award was given to him for his work in establishing relationship equity. This concept is now a living reality in our modern times as a result of truth and reality, which have made the impact that this philosophy has had on the world something that is mind-boggling. Dr. Femi has created a relationship model that has the potential to change the world by bringing together science and spirituality. His book, The Five Pillars of Relationship Equity, is the first of its kind anywhere in the world. It contains information that is both pertinent and supported by science and spirituality. This book is essential for any organization that deals with families or family development because it is the authoritative voice of World Civility. Dr. Femi is truly a trailblazer when it comes to the discovery of new information about relationships. This literary masterpiece provides the tools necessary to mend broken relationships and build healthy ones. As the global leader of civility across the world, I would recommend this book to any organization that is interested in motivating people to advance further and live the lives of their dreams. I feel incredibly honored to be asked to write the forward for this book.

HRH Dr. Clyde Rivers

Okogyeman Kobina Amissah I

World Civility Leader, President of iChange Nations, and a world-renowned leadership trainer who has been training leaders for over 25 years.

Preface

The importance of pursuing equity and fairness in romantic relationships is frequently disregarded, even though this topic has been debated for a considerable amount of time in the context of professional relationships. Romantic relationships, in contrast to business transactions, involve two individuals who voluntarily choose to embark on a journey together that may last for the rest of their lives. This is not a simple business transaction in any way.

The foundation of a healthy romantic relationship is a shared commitment to cultivating a welcoming and equitable environment for both partners, which in turn promotes happiness and a sense of fulfillment. On the other hand, it is not unusual for some romantic partnerships to feature an imbalance, in which one partner derives a greater benefit from the relationship than the other. This disparity results in dissatisfaction and power dynamics, both of which have the potential to negatively impact the quality of the relationship.

Throughout history, women have been subjected to discrimination within the context of romantic relationships. This is because societal expectations have traditionally relegated them to the role of primary caregiver, with men being expected to shoulder the responsibility of financially supporting their families. Nevertheless, as time went on, women eventually achieved financial independence and began contributing alongside men to the income of their families. Because of this shift, there is now a complicated interplay of roles and expectations, which has led to power struggles as well as confusion for men.

The cultivation of equity becomes essential to the development of a romantic relationship that is both harmonious and successful. Couples can navigate the complexities of modern relationships and acknowledge each partner's contributions and needs if they make fairness and balance a priority in their interactions with one another. The adoption of equity helps to cultivate a deeper level of understanding, respect, and shared responsibilities, which in turn helps to cultivate a relationship that is built on equality and fulfillment.

Introduction

The traditional notions of gender roles and power dynamics have been challenged in the dynamic landscape of relationships, giving rise to a need for re-evaluation and adaptation. As society has evolved, with women increasingly taking on roles in the corporate and entrepreneurial realms once dominated by men, household dynamics have undergone a significant transformation. This shifting paradigm has disrupted the conventional understanding of masculinity and femininity, leading to a power struggle and competition between partners instead of collaboration and mutual support. The crux of the issue lies in the difficulty men face in navigating this new era as they grapple with unlearning long-held beliefs about marriage and embracing the gifts and advancements of modern women. Consequently, this conflict has impacted the overall satisfaction and harmony of relationships.

Relationship equity emerges as a guiding principle, emphasizing fairness, power balance, and utilizing individual gifts and talents to propel personal and familial growth. Achieving equity entails a sense of reciprocity, where investments in love, respect, and honor are met with equal measure. This approach avoids double standards and ensures both partners feel appropriately valued and rewarded.

Relationship equity is not synonymous with absolute equality; it recognizes that responsibilities and roles may differ based on individual strengths and biological attributes. For instance, a man cannot breastfeed or carry a baby in the womb because he's not naturally gifted with those resources.

"Wives, submit yourselves to your own husbands as you do to the Lord. For the husband is the head of the wife, just as Christ is the head of the church, his body, of which he is the Savior. Now as the church submits to Christ, so also wives should submit to their husbands in everything." Ephesians 5:22–24 NIV.

Establishing a relationship hierarchy, as God has ordained, does not justify authoritarian rule or subjugation. Instead, it calls for a mutual appreciation and recognition of each partner's unique contributions, fostering a harmonious and fulfilling partnership. God establishes a hierarchical structure within the home to ensure order and harmony. Recognizing that a woman is not a mere servant but a valuable helpmate is essential. She is not a maid but an aid, contributing meaningfully beyond physical labor. Women bring more than their bodies and natural nurturing instincts to the table. Similarly, men are not limited to being hunters, providers, and protectors. Each individual possesses unique gifts, talents, and ideas that should be acknowledged and valued, maximizing personal and family interests.

Chapter One

Studies On Relationship Equity

Relationship equity, defined as the fair distribution of responsibilities, resources, and decision-making within a partnership, is crucial for maintaining satisfaction and stability. This comprehensive report examines various studies that shed light on the relationship between gender roles, parenting, and relationship equity. The findings highlight the importance of practicing fairness and support in relationships and provide insights into the challenges faced by couples in achieving relationship equity.

Impact of Gender Roles on Relationship Satisfaction:
The Ruppanner, L., Brandén, M., and Turunen, J. (2018) study reveals that women who bear a disproportionate amount of housework are more likely to experience dissatisfaction in their relationships and consider breaking up. The study emphasizes the significance of an equitable division of domestic responsibilities to ensure relationship satisfaction and stability.

It also indicates that women who perform more housework are less likely to be satisfied with their relationships and are more likely to consider breaking up. These types of relationships are also more likely to dissolve. The dissatisfaction experienced among couples is dependent on women being under-benefitted in domestic division arrangements.

Women who perform more housework are less likely to be satisfied with their relationships and are more likely to consider breaking up.

The Pandemic's Effect on Relationship Equity:

The COVID-19 pandemic has magnified the challenges faced by women in maintaining a work-life balance. The 2020 'Women in the Workplace' study indicates that women, especially mothers, face increased pressure when juggling parenting and work responsibilities. McKinsey & Company (2020) reported that the pandemic has led one in four women to contemplate leaving the workforce or downshifting their careers, highlighting the unequal burden placed on women in dual-career couples with children.

The pandemic also has a near-immediate effect on women's satisfaction. More women than men experience their careers being tested during the pandemic as they struggle to juggle parenting with work. According to the 2020 'Women in the Workplace' study, despite companies' efforts to support employees during the crisis, women feel exhausted, burned out, and under more pressure than men. Mothers bear more of the burden at home than fathers. While the children were home, the mothers had to stay with them, teach them, and feed them while still having to manage the feeling of needing to be at work at all hours, or "always on."

Parenthood and relationship satisfaction:

Keizer and Schenk's (2012) research explores the impact of

becoming parents on relationship satisfaction. The study reveals that changes in work hours and household labor significantly influence the satisfaction levels of individuals and their partners. The findings demonstrate that unfairness within a relationship, whether related to parenting or other areas, can lead to dissatisfaction and strain the partnership.

McKinsey & Company (2020) reported that one in four women considers leaving the workforce or downshifting their careers, versus one in five men. It was mainly noted, especially among parents of kids under ten. The rate at which women considered leaving was ten percentage points higher than for men. The study further revealed that women in dual-career couples with children reported increased time spent on domestic responsibilities since the pandemic.

Beyond Household Chores: Examining Relationship Equity

The conclusions drawn from these studies underscore the significance of support and fairness in maintaining relationship satisfaction. While the division of household chores is an important aspect, it is essential to explore other pillars of relationship equity as well. This highlights the need to examine and address fairness in various areas of the relationship beyond domestic responsibilities.

While the division of household chores is an important aspect, it is essential to explore other pillars of relationship equity as well.

Whenever there is a change in the dynamic of couples, such as parenting a child, dissatisfaction is likely to rise if there is no plan to share responsibilities because the bulk of the work will shift towards one partner rather than both. Keizer, R., and Schenk, N. (2012) investigated how becoming a parent affects women's and men's relationship satisfaction within couples and how changes in work hours and hours spent on household labor affect an individual's or their spouse's relationship satisfaction across the transition to parenthood. The authors selected 689 employed, childless couples living together during the observation. The result revealed that work hours and household labor had some effect on individuals' and spouses' relationship satisfaction. This study proved that it does not matter if you are a parent-child couple or a couple with no child; as long as you are in a relationship, unfairness can be experienced in different areas of the relationship.

The conclusions of many of the studies show that a lack of support at home creates dissatisfaction. The findings also influence the decision to examine different pillars or areas of relationship equity that measure fairness in the relationship beyond the division of household chores. Hence, this birthed the five pillars of relationship equity that can help couples examine their relationships and practice fairness where necessary. However, before we dive into the five pillars, it is essential to highlight that the effective practice of relationship equity requires the power of two (husband and wife).

The studies on relationship equity emphasize the importance of a fair division of responsibilities and resources within a partnership. Gender disparities in household chores and the added challenges of parenting can contribute to dissatisfaction and strain in relationships. Recognizing the need for fairness, support, and open communication, the report introduces the concept of the five pillars of relationship equity as a framework for couples to evaluate and cultivate fairness in their relationships.

It is crucial for couples to proactively address relationship equity, acknowledging the power of two individuals working together to create a fair and fulfilling partnership. By practicing fairness and support in all aspects of their relationship, couples can enhance relationship satisfaction, foster mutual understanding, and promote long-term relationship stability.

Chapter Two

The Power Of Two

Deuteronomy 32:30 asks, "How could one man chase a thousand, or two put ten thousand to flight, unless their rock had sold them, unless the LORD had given them up?" (NIV).

"Two are better than one because the return on their labor is greater when there are two of them. If one of them were to fall down, the other could help the one who fell up. However, I feel sorry for anyone who trips and has no one to help them up." (Ecclesiastes 4:9–10 NIV).

An example of the power of two in relationships can be seen in a successful business partnership where two individuals complement each other's skills and work together towards a common goal, resulting in greater success than if they were working alone. For instance, Steve Jobs and Steve Wozniak co-founded Apple Inc. in 1976, with Jobs being the visionary and Wozniak being the technical genius behind the company's products. Together, they built a company that revolutionized the technology industry and became one of the most valuable companies in the world. Without each other's unique talents and abilities, they may not have achieved such great success. The power of one partner enhances and magnifies the power of the other, but this effect is only there so long as the partners continue to work together.

There is something intriguing about the concept of the "power of two" in our society.

It can be seen in various aspects of life, from romantic relationships to business partnerships. When two individuals come together and combine their strengths, they can often achieve more than they could alone. With my wife and me, there are some things I am naturally gifted in that she is not, and vice versa. Nevertheless, this still strengthens our union. I counsel people on relationships; this is my calling and my profession, but my wife is an event coordinator, and she coordinates weddings. When I have a relationship event, she coordinates: she comes up with how to design the event, who should sit at the table, the gifts to be distributed, and so on. We both go about our various gifts this way. Also, when she plans a wedding for her client, I officiate at the wedding. This way, God combines our gifts. I talk, and she coordinates, though she sometimes gets to talk too. Another area is the church. I play drums, and my wife is in the protocol unit, where she attends to pastors. Here, we both serve in our local church with our God-given talents to advance God's kingdom. We go to church together, but she may have a reason to stay longer because of the department where she serves. So I wait for her, no matter how long it takes. However, when we started having children, I would take them home so they wouldn't have to wait long. While at home with the children, I prepare their meals, prepare them for school the next day, bathe them, and tuck them into bed. Meanwhile, my wife is in church, attending to the pastor. You may wonder how I have coped here; it is through love and understanding. I allow my wife to use her gift to advance God's kingdom in church while I help her do the necessary chores at home. This understanding binds us together.

Maintaining a balance of power and mutual respect in any partnership, whether romantic, professional, or otherwise, is important.

However, the power of the two can also be a double-edged sword. If one partner becomes dominant or controlling, the dynamic can quickly become unhealthy and oppressive. Maintaining a balance of power and mutual respect in any partnership, whether romantic, professional, or otherwise, is important. As we continue to navigate the complexities of gender dynamics in our society, we must remain mindful. This refers to a singular, self-contained link that can develop between two individuals and produce a distinct catalytic spark.

- The concept of synergy in teamwork and how it relates to the power of two individuals working together is evident in both the Bible and in successful business partnerships. By combining their strengths and supporting each other, two people can achieve greater success than they would on their own. The story of Apple Inc. is just one example of how two people can change the world when they work together towards a common goal.

- The importance of a support system in achieving goals and overcoming obstacles, especially when one person falls or faces challenges alone, cannot be overemphasized. This support system can come from a partner, friend, or mentor who can provide encouragement, advice, and assistance when needed. By having someone to rely on during difficult times, individuals can stay motivated and focused on their goals, ultimately achieving greater success. The power of two in relationships is not just about complimenting each other's skills but also about providing emotional support and encouragement to help each other reach their full potential. It is so unfortunate that these days, couples find it difficult to support each other. What goes on in most homes is paranoia, suspicion, and competition. It's so bad that even when one couple helps the other, there is no appreciation from the receiving end. The order of the day is an entitlement mentality, and this has led to chaos in most homes, leading them to fall apart. I remember a time in 2019 when I felt the calling to quit my job and go into full-time ministry and entrepreneurship. That year was tough because I couldn't contribute as much as I used to, but my wife could shoulder the responsibilities. There was a time when my wife had an American credit card. She put me on that credit card. She was questioned by the company about putting my name on it and if she was sure she wanted to do that, and she said yes, she wanted to. Now putting me under the credit card increases my credit score, and in America, your credit score matters. I can also use a credit card to buy what I need to buy without my wife's permission, and this made me appreciate my wife more because it is an act of giving that will raise eyebrows. You may be wondering if I reciprocated. Yes, I did. This happened on our "9th wedding anniversary. By then, I was back on my feet financially, so I realized that my wife needed a car. We went to a car dealer and spotted a Mercedes G wagon. She drove it around, and the next day, while going back to the car dealer, I had a conversation in my success and well-being.

- The idea that faith or spirituality can provide a foundation for the power of two by giving individuals guidance and motivation to work together towards common goals. Faith or spirituality can provide individuals with a sense of purpose and meaning, which can be a powerful motivator for achieving shared goals. By having a shared belief system, individuals can also find comfort and support in each other during difficult times. This can lead to a deeper connection and understanding between partners, ultimately strengthening their relationship and increasing their chances of success. Faith or spirituality can also provide a sense of accountability and responsibility towards each other, encouraging individuals to work towards their goals with integrity and commitment.

The most important thing is that you can communicate your feelings to your partner in a way they understand. I think the best way is to be honest about what you want and don't want. If you can do this, it will be easier for both of you to work out how best to mind with God about how to pay for the car, and God told me I would pay with money earned from my business. When my wife asked, I told her I would pay, and there was the shock and joy that followed. I was able to get my wife a car! Note this: In my time of need, she was there for me, and she did this by obeying God. So, when I also spotted her need and was able to provide it, I did. By doing that, we were able to support each other. Note that it wasn't that I was paying her back, but I was appreciating her. We both love doing things for each other.

⊙ How the strength of relationships between people can impact success, productivity, and overall well-being in marriage, and how equity and communication are key components in maintaining a healthy relationship. When both partners feel valued and heard, they are more likely to work together towards common goals and overcome challenges together. A strong relationship can also increase happiness and fulfillment in both personal and professional aspects of life. It is important to prioritize and invest in relationships, as they can significantly impact one's overall meet each other's needs.

Q: How do I know if my partner is honest with me?

You can tell if your partner is being honest with you by looking at their actions and words. If they are being honest, they will be open and willing to talk about their feelings, thoughts, and opinions. They will also be willing to listen to yours. If your partner is not honest with you, they may try to hide their feelings or thoughts from you.

you can communicate your feelings to your partner in a way they understand. I think the best way is to be honest about what you want and don't want.

"As iron sharpens iron, so one person sharpens the other" (Proverbs 27:17, New International Version). This highlights the significance of collaboration and support in achieving success. The power of two individuals working together can lead to revolutionary ideas and groundbreaking achievements. The importance of relationships and faith in providing guidance and motivation cannot be underestimated. Couples can engage in teamwork by:

- Further exploring the meaning and importance of Ecclesiastes 4:9–10 in daily life, especially in a world where individualism is often prioritized over teamwork in relationships.

- Analyzing case studies or real-life examples of successful partnerships and how they were able to achieve more together than alone For example, two entrepreneurs with complementary skills and shared values can start a successful business together. By collaborating and supporting each other, they can overcome challenges and bring innovative ideas to the table. Similarly, in a romantic relationship, partners who are honest and open with each other can build trust and deepen their connection, leading to a stronger bond and a happier life together.

- Discussing the role of communication and trust in building strong relationships that can withstand marriage challenges and setbacks For instance, if my wife and I regularly communicate our needs and concerns to each other and actively work to build trust, we can weather financial difficulties or other setbacks in our marriage. By supporting each other emotionally and being transparent in our actions, we strengthen our relationship and deepen our love for each other. I would like to go back to how my wife supported the family when I was financially down. She did this without expecting anything in return from me; she placed my name on the credit card because she trusted me. Most couples don't trust each other enough to do this. They are not even honest with each other about their finances. Most homes are destroyed today because of issues with finances. The best is to be honest with each other and have a positive mind and attitude towards each other.

- Exploring different support systems, including friends, family, mentors, and coaches. These support systems can play a crucial role in helping individuals and couples navigate challenges and achieve their goals. Friends and family can provide emotional support and a listening ear, while mentors and coaches can offer guidance and expertise in a specific area. By surrounding themselves with a diverse group of supportive individuals, people can build a strong network to help them overcome obstacles and succeed in all areas of their lives.

The New International Version of the Bible asks, "*Do two walk together unless they have agreed to do so?"* (Amos 3:3)

This verse emphasizes the importance of shared goals and values in any partnership or relationship. It is not enough to work together; rather, there must be a mutual understanding and agreement on what is being worked towards. This idea can be applied to both personal and professional relationships, as having a clear direction and purpose can lead to greater success and fulfillment. Additionally, it is important to regularly assess and communicate these goals and values in order to maintain a strong and healthy partnership.

Do two walk together unless they have agreed to do so?"* *(Amos 3:3)

The Bible makes a point of emphasizing the significance of collaboration between individuals and the greater impact that can be made as a result of the combined efforts of those involved. We can observe the significance of the partnership at a number of different institutions. For instance, a government that is able to collaborate and work together with other nations can achieve greater diplomatic success. Similarly, businesses that foster a collaborative work environment often see increased productivity and innovation. The Bible's emphasis on collaboration also extends to the spiritual realm, where believers are encouraged to unite in fellowship and support each other on their faith journeys. Additionally, the verses above highlight the importance of helping others in need and building relationships based on mutual respect and trust. Finally, when comparing how various communities have collaborated throughout history, king-led governments will always have a queen, whereas presidents and vice presidents lead our contemporary governments. A governor will typically have a deputy governor, just as a ship captain will typically have a co-captain and a pilot will typically have a co-pilot. All of these demonstrate the importance of striking a balance and taking shared responsibility. When one of the leaders becomes exhausted, the other leader can step up and take charge.

The power of two people, and more specifically, the power of a husband and wife working together, is a tremendous force capable of bringing about incredible results in various facets of life. However, collaboration is a key aspect of success in both the workplace and the spiritual realm. The Bible emphasizes the importance of coming together in fellowship and supporting each other, as well as helping those in need and building relationships based on mutual respect and trust. Looking at historical and modern examples, it is clear that shared responsibility and balance are crucial for effective leadership. My wife and I collaborate; we work together, we fellowship together, and it has brought about incredible results in our marriage. It has exuded beauty in our marriage.

When two people decide to work together on a project, their individual capabilities, skills, and strengths can combine to produce a synergy that is greater than what either of them could accomplish on their own.

Furthermore, the collaboration also allows for diverse perspectives and ideas to be brought to the table, leading to more creative solutions and better decision-making. It also fosters a sense of community and belonging, which are essential for personal and professional growth.

Working together fosters a sense of community and belonging, which are essential for personal and professional growth.

Hence, it is important to note that collaboration does not mean sacrificing individuality or compromising one's values. Rather, it is about finding common ground and working towards a shared goal while respecting each other's differences. In today's fast-paced and interconnected world, collaboration is more important than ever, and those who embrace it are more likely to achieve success and make a positive impact in their communities. *For example*, a husband-and-wife team who both have expertise in marketing and finance can collaborate to start a successful small business. They can combine their knowledge and skills to create a strong brand strategy, develop effective financial plans, and execute marketing campaigns that resonate with their target audience. By working together, they can also support each other through the challenges of entrepreneurship and build a business that reflects their shared values and goals. After I became a full-time entrepreneur, I had a large sum of money, and my wife advised me that we should invest it, which I obeyed, and we made a huge profit! I will always pray for blessings for my wife and her wise counsel.

Working together as a team in a marriage or other committed relationship enables spouses to pool both their tangible and intangible resources, which enables them to overcome challenges and pursue common goals more effectively. They are able to tackle tasks and responsibilities in a manner that is more efficient and effective because they leverage each other's strengths and compensate for each other's weaknesses.

The decisions that my wife and I make together always have a significant bearing on our individual lives. Every time we cooperate, we offer each other support, encouragement, and companionship, all of which are enhanced. During trying times, we are able to lean on each other, dividing the load and finding comfort in the fact that we have been through similar situations. Because of this unity, our bond is strengthened, and it also nurtures a profound emotional connection and intimacy.

The power of two people working together extends beyond the realm of personal satisfaction into a variety of spheres, including but not limited to the realms of parenting, household management, and financial decision-making. When partners actively contribute and collaborate, they create an environment that is balanced and harmonious. In this environment, responsibilities are shared, decisions are made jointly, and the voice of each individual is valued. This joint effort makes things easier for both parties involved and ensures that each person feels a sense of ownership over the results and has some financial stake in them. I remember a time when my wife was coordinating an event in Mexico for one of her clients (it was a birthday party), which was on a weekend. I had an event on Saturday. I wanted to surprise her at that event. This was my way of supporting her because we love to support each other and surprise each other. I had just a thousand dollars on me, which was enough to board a flight. I got there on a Thursday and found a way to get to my wife's room through one of her friends who was working with her. She was really surprised, and we spent the evening together with friends who told me that she had been stressed and strained, but my presence eased the tension she was facing. I spent just a night there, but my presence made a positive impact on my wife because I was there to support her.

In addition, the power generated when two people collaborate on a project transcends the bounds of their relationships with one another. They have the potential to make a significant impact on their community, society, and even the world at large when acting as a unified front. They are able to embark on meaningful projects, advocate for the causes they believe in, and inspire others through their shared efforts, thanks to the fact that they have combined their talents, resources, and passions.

Overall, the power of two people working together is immense and extends far beyond personal satisfaction. It creates a balanced and harmonious environment where responsibilities are shared, decisions are made jointly, and each individual's voice is valued. This joint effort not only makes things easier for both parties involved but also has the potential to make a significant impact on their community, society, and the world at large. When I arrived in Mexico to support my wife, there was a feeling of joy and happiness that the people around me felt. It made the job easier for my wife. I was willing to spend my last to support her and go back to Maryland for my program.

Nevertheless, to tap into the combined potential of two people, there must be transparent communication, mutual respect, and a willingness to cooperate. It necessitates recognizing and appreciating the unique qualities and viewpoints that each person holds, as well as being willing to compromise and finding points of agreement. The husband and wife can tap into their collective power to create a fulfilling and purposeful life together by cultivating a culture of teamwork and shared decision-making.

In the past, I worked as a cybersecurity consultant for the United States Embassy in four different countries, including Vietnam, Cambodia, Timor Leste, and Indonesia. This job required extensive travel. The journey was broken up into two parts, with a stop in between each section. My wife initially gave her permission for me to participate in the first phase of the activity, but she was apprehensive about the second one.

However, through open and honest communication, we were able to discuss our concerns and come up with a plan that worked for both of us. This allowed me to continue with my job while also addressing my wife's worries. By working together, we were able to overcome this challenge and strengthen our relationship. It is through these types of collaborations that we can achieve great things and make a positive impact on the world around us. Overall, my experience as a cybersecurity consultant for the United States Embassy was challenging but rewarding. Through open communication and collaboration with my wife, we were able to overcome the difficulties of extensive travel and strengthen our relationship. I believe that working together and addressing concerns is essential to achieving success and making a positive impact on the world.

In case you are wondering what I actually did to convince my wife to agree for the second trip, I persuaded her by pointing out the positive aspects of the solution. She was exhausted and unable to sleep because our son was still nursing, which was the cause of the problem. I explained that if we took the trip together, our son would be able to transition off of breastfeeding by the time we got back, which would allow her to get more rest.

In addition, I guaranteed that I would use the money I made from the trip to purchase a brand new truck for her. I drew her attention to these particular benefits during our conversation. Through persuasion and highlighting the positive aspects of the solution, I was able to convince my wife to take the trip with me, which ultimately led to her getting more rest and our son transitioning off of breastfeeding. I am grateful for the success we achieved through collaboration.

In terms of what we would gain as a couple, I mentioned that my wife and I hadn't been on vacation since the birth of our child and that this trip might provide us with the much-needed opportunity to take a break. Because our wedding anniversary fell during our trip, we were able to celebrate it during our time away. In addition, it would be another memorable experience for both of us to add to our collection of travel adventures across the globe, and it would bring us closer together as a couple. Overall, the benefits of taking this trip were numerous, and I am glad that we were able to work together to make it happen.

As a consequence of this, she quickly agreed, and the time that we spent together in Cambodia was very enjoyable. Because our son was no longer dependent on my wife's breast milk, she was able to get better sleep. Additionally, with the money I made from the trip, I was able to afford to buy her a truck. The preceding example demonstrates how well we can cooperate as a couple. We decided to take a trip to Cambodia, which would provide us with a much-needed break since we hadn't been on vacation since the birth of our child. Celebrating our wedding anniversary during the trip would make it even more memorable, and it would bring us closer together as a couple. The benefits of the trip were numerous, and we were able to work together to make it happen. The time we spent together in Cambodia was enjoyable, and my wife was able to get better sleep.

As earlier stated in this chapter, my wife makes use of the natural talent she possesses for wedding planning, and I make use of the skills I possess to officiate the weddings she plans and offer relationship advice to the newlyweds. Overall, we demonstrate a strong ability to work together and support each other's goals and passions. From taking a much-needed vacation to utilizing our individual skills to create a successful business, they prioritize their relationship and strive for mutual success.

Our collaboration has allowed us to reach a wider audience and offer more comprehensive advice to those seeking to improve their relationships. It's amazing to see how our individual strengths can come together to create something greater than ourselves. This approach has not only strengthened our relationship but also our professional lives. We are grateful for each other's support and look forward to continuing to work together towards our shared goals. When it comes to the organization of relationship seminars, my wife plays a pivotal role in the coordination of a support team. We can increase our productivity as a group and get more done as a result of combining our various skills and advantages.

The ability of two people to put each other's needs ahead of their own is a key factor in determining how much power they wield together. For example, my wife and I organize relationship events for singles and couples to strengthen their relationships. I focus on delivering the content while my wife manages the logistics, such as guests' accommodations, meals, assemble supporting teams, and sometimes speaks. With our combined efforts, we are able to provide a seamless experience for our attendees and receive rave reviews. Our ability to work together allow us to create something that is greater than the sum of its parts. When pursuing personal goals, one ought to take into account how those goals can be of benefit to both oneself and others. When pursuing personal goals, it is essential to take a momentary break and consider the following three important questions: (a) What advantages will I get out of this? (b) In what ways will my partner profit from this? (c) What are the advantages for us as a couple? We are not utilizing the power of two to its full potential if we confine our attention solely to our successes without also taking into account those of our collaborators.

The ability of two people to put each other's needs ahead of their own is a key factor in determining how much power they wield together.

In the course of my work as a counselor, I frequently come across clients who are having difficulty winning their partner's support for the personal goals they have set for themselves. I help them understand, through counseling, that their partner's lack of support is not due to a lack of willingness but rather a lack of communication regarding how the goal can benefit both individuals and strengthen their relationship. Therefore, it is important to communicate effectively with our partners and involve them in our personal goals, as this can lead to a stronger relationship and greater success for both individuals. Collaboration and consideration for others can lead to a more fulfilling and successful life. I do this by pointing out how the goal can benefit both of them individually and how it can strengthen their relationship. I was able to effectively explain to my wife the benefits that she would experience personally as well as the positive impact that it would have on us as a couple, including the growth opportunities that it would provide for my career, by using the example that I shared about traveling to Cambodia with my wife. It was much simpler for her to support the itinerary after adopting an inclusive mentality and focusing on the benefits that would accrue to both parties.

In summary, it is important to involve our partners in our personal goals and communicate effectively with them.

Collaboration and consideration for others can lead to a more fulfilling and successful life. By highlighting the benefits that both individuals can gain from achieving personal goals, we can strengthen our relationships and achieve greater success. I shared earlier a personal example of how my wife and I effectively communicated the benefits of a shared goal, resulting in a successful trip to Cambodia. By involving partners in personal goals and highlighting the benefits for both individuals, we can lead more fulfilling and successful lives.

The transformative power of two people, and in particular, the power of a husband and wife working together, can lead to personal development, harmonious relationships, and significant accomplishments. Ultimately, it is important to remember that our personal goals do not exist in a vacuum, and by involving our partners and communicating effectively, we can create a more fulfilling and successful life for ourselves and our loved ones. They can navigate the challenges of life, achieve shared goals, and experience the profound joy of walking the journey together because they leverage their combined strengths, support each other's endeavors, and collaborate as equal partners. Involving our partners in our personal goals and communicating effectively with them is crucial for a fulfilling and successful life.

Collaboration and consideration for others can also lead to personal development, harmonious relationships, and significant accomplishments. The transformative power of two people, especially a husband and wife working together, can create a strong foundation for navigating life's challenges and achieving shared goals. By leveraging our combined strengths and supporting each other's endeavors, we can experience the profound joy of walking the journey together.

When we acknowledge and accept the strength that comes from working together as a team, we are able to unlock the enormous potential that lies inside collaborative endeavors. When we work together, we are capable of accomplishing much more than any of us could ever do on our own. The power of two is a powerful force for good in our world today.

Collaboration allows us to combine our unique strengths, skills, and perspectives to tackle complex problems and achieve our goals. It fosters creativity, innovation, and mutual respect, and it enables us to learn from one another and grow both personally and professionally. Moreover, collaboration promotes a sense of belonging and community as we work towards a common purpose and support each other along the way.

Let us not forget the wisdom that may be gleaned from these passages and instead look for ways to build meaningful relationships with one another by encouraging one another, honing our abilities, and working toward the same objectives.

The power of two people working together has the potential to bring about great change and extraordinary accomplishments. This force should not be underestimated. For example, medical researchers working together can combine their knowledge and expertise to develop new treatments and cures for diseases. By sharing data and insights, they can accelerate the pace of discovery and make breakthroughs that would never have been possible for a single individual or team. This collaboration has led to advances in fields such as cancer research, genetic engineering, and neuroscience, which have improved the lives of countless people around the world.

When couples collaborate and cooperate, there is potential strength and effectiveness that can be achieved. They have the opportunity to provide each other with emotional support and understanding. They can offer comfort, encouragement, and a safe space to share their thoughts and feelings. This mutual support can contribute to increased resilience and well-being for them.

Couples can align their goals and aspirations, which will create a shared vision for their future. To achieve this, they can work together to achieve common objectives as they build their family together, pursue their careers and ambitions, and create a fulfilling life together. When they have a shared sense of purpose, it can enhance motivation and increase success in their relationship. As a couple, you can always rely on each other during difficult times. If my wife had been selfish when I decided to quit my job and venture into entrepreneurship, life would have been so difficult for me. On the other hand, my wife single-handedly supported the family and even got a credit card with my name on it, which made me creditworthy. With this, I had a sense of belonging as I basked in her love and support.

It is important to note that the power of two as a couple relies on healthy communication, mutual respect, and a commitment to work together. When couples nurture these, they are able to harness their collective strength and create a fulfilling and successful relationship.

I pray that we may see the transforming force of the power of two in both our own lives and the world around us, and that we may do so with open arms.

Chapter Three

Five Pillars Of Relationship Equity

Relationship equity refers to the balance and fairness in a romantic relationship in which both partners feel valued and acknowledged for their contributions and needs. It is the concept of maintaining a sense of equality and reciprocity in the relationship, ensuring that both partners feel they are receiving their fair share of love, support, respect, and effort. In a relationship, equity refers to the situation in which responsibilities, decision-making authority, emotional support, and resources are shared between the two partners in a manner considered fair by both parties. It goes beyond merely trading one favor for another and instead focuses on forming a partnership that benefits both parties and creates a sense of fulfillment.

(A) Power Balance Do both husbands and wives have an equal voice in their relationship or is one partner deemed more powerful based on gender? Let us challenge the notion that gender equals power. If we believe that gender determines strength, we essentially endorse the idea that one gender holds dominion over the other, potentially leading to an imbalance of power in relationships. However, the truth is that humans were created to have authority over everything except each other (English Standard Version Bible, 2016, Gen. 1:28). God intended for marriages to be founded on mutual respect and shared authority. Both the husband and wife are co-founders of their relationship, with the husband assuming the role of leadership for the sake of organization and order.

Power balance is a fundamental aspect of relationship equity. Every relationship has a power dynamic," which refers to the ability to influence or control one's partner or the relationship itself. When power is unequally distributed, one partner may exert more control, make decisions that primarily benefit themselves, disregard their partner's needs or opinions, or engage in controlling or abusive behavior. This imbalance can foster resentment, frustration, and mistrust within the relationship.

When power is balanced, both partners have an equal say in decision-making and possess a similar ability to shape the course of the relationship.

Conversely, when power is balanced, both partners have an equal say in decision-making and possess a similar ability to shape the course of the relationship. Power balance fosters a sense of equity where each partner's needs and opinions hold equal value and are given due consideration.

A balanced power dynamic requires ongoing communication, compromise, and a willingness to listen and understand each other's perspectives. It also involves challenging societal norms or beliefs and perpetuating unequal power distribution through

traditional gender roles or cultural expectations.
A harmonious and equitable relationship necessitates a balanced power dynamic where partners contribute to each other's growth and well-being. If wives are solely focused on supporting their husbands (English Standard Version Bible, 2016, Gen. 2:18), who will support and nurture the wives in the visions and dreams that God has instilled within them? Marriage demands interdependence, as highlighted in the scripture: "Nevertheless, in the Lord, the woman is not independent of man, nor man of woman; for as woman was made from man, so man is born of woman, and all things are from God" (English Standard Version Bible, 2016, I Corinthians 11:11–12). Each person relies on the power inherent in others. No individual possesses superior power over another. The accurate measure of power lies in individuals' unique gifts from birth, knowledge, value, and skill sets.

Examples of power balance in an equitable relationship

1. Shared decision-making: Both partners have an equal say in important decisions that affect the relationship, such as financial planning, significant purchases, and life goals.

2. Balanced responsibilities: Both partners take on an equal share of responsibilities at home, such as housework, childcare, and cooking.

3. Mutual respect: Each partner values the other's opinions, feelings, and needs and works to meet them fairly and respectfully.

4. Open communication: Both partners communicate openly and honestly, listening actively and working to understand each other's perspectives.

5. Equal access to resources: Both partners have access to the resources they need to thrive, whether financial resources, time, or emotional support.

6. Mutual support: Both partners offer support, whether emotional support during difficult times or practical help with day-to-day tasks.

7. Shared accountability: Both partners take responsibility for their actions and work together to resolve conflicts

fairly and respectfully.

Fostering a power balance in relationships is vital to establishing equity and respect. It involves recognizing and challenging existing power dynamics, valuing each partner's voice and contributions, and working together to create a relationship founded on mutual support and understanding. When power is shared equally, both partners can thrive, and the relationship can flourish healthily and harmoniously.

(B) Gifting. When we talk about gifting in the context of a relationship, we're not necessarily referring to material gifts like flowers, jewelry, or other tangible items (although these can certainly be part of it). Instead, we're referring to using our natural gifts and talents to support and nurture our partners.

Everyone is born with a unique gift or talent bestowed upon them by a higher power. The Scripture affirms this truth, as God revealed to Jeremiah that he was anointed as a prophet even before his formation in his mother's womb (English Standard Version Bible, 2016, Jeremiah 1:5). It is essential to recognize that just as men have the opportunity to advance in their careers and pursue their passions through their talents, women should be equally encouraged to embrace and utilize their God-given gifts outside of their familial roles. The virtuous woman described in Proverbs 31:10–31 ESV exemplifies this balance beautifully, as she successfully managed her clothing business while also tending to the needs of her family.

It is essential to recognize that just as men have the opportunity to advance in their careers and pursue their passions through their talents, women should be equally encouraged to embrace and utilize their God-given gifts outside of their familial roles.

Unfortunately, the COVID-19 pandemic brought to light the challenges faced by women, particularly mothers, who considered leaving the workforce and relinquishing their gifts and talents due to the lack of support and assistance from their husbands at home (McKinsey & Company, 2020). Traditions and cultural practices have often confined women to domestic responsibilities, pigeonholing them into the roles of cooking and childcare. Marriage should never be viewed as a woman's ultimate achievement or sole purpose. Every woman is born with a destiny, unique gifts, and purpose that extend far beyond the bounds of marriage. If a woman possesses the talent and potential to run a business or pursue her calling, her husband should empower, support, and encourage her in these endeavors. A woman's success in her chosen field does not diminish a man's light or diminish his position as a man. Authentic leadership involves empowering and uplifting those under one's care. We are designed to assist one another in fulfilling our purposes and destinies, transcending the confines of marriage alone.

When both partners in a relationship recognize and harness their natural gifts to support and nurture each other, it creates a harmonious balance and a deep sense of equity. For instance, if one partner excels at organization and planning, they may take charge of scheduling appointments and managing the household calendar. On the other hand, if the other partner possesses culinary skills, they might be responsible for preparing nourishing meals for the family. By valuing and leveraging each other's unique gifts, both partners feel genuinely appreciated and esteemed for their distinct contributions to the relationship. Such practice fosters a sense of equity and mutual respect, as both individuals are empowered to make meaningful contributions and help each other achieve their goals and aspirations.

This mutual investment in each other's growth and fulfillment becomes a powerful catalyst for building and sustaining a healthy and equitable relationship between husband and wife. Nevertheless, it is crucial to recognize that only some couples find it effortless to identify and harness each other's gifts to nurture and cultivate their relationship. Those couples practice open communication, understanding, and a shared commitment to promoting each other's growth and well-being. The couples can discover the true beauty and power within their shared equity.

Challenges couples face with the idea of using their natural gifts and talents to support and nurture each other:

1. Different interests and talents: Partners may have different natural gifts and talents that do not necessarily align,

making it challenging to support and nurture each other in a way that feels equitable and fulfilling for both partners.

2. Unbalanced expectations: If one partner has a particular talent or gift, the other partner may feel pressure to provide support and nurture in a different area, creating an unbalanced division of labor and potentially causing resentment.

3. Fear of dependency: Some partners may fear becoming too dependent on their partner's natural gifts and talents, leading to feelings of vulnerability and insecurity.

4. Difficulty identifying natural gifts and talents: It may be difficult for partners to identify their natural gifts and talents or to recognize and appreciate the gifts and talents of their partner.

Couples need open and honest communication about their interests and strengths. Partners can work together to identify each other's natural gifts and talents and find ways to support and nurture each other in a way that feels equitable and fulfilling for both partners. Couples can also explore new interests and talents together and be open to learning and growing alongside each other. It is essential for partners to recognize and appreciate each other's unique strengths and contributions and to avoid placing expectations or judgments on each other based on traditional gender roles or societal expectations.

How gifting can play a role in relationship equity

1. Sharing responsibilities: One-way gifting can support relationship equity by helping balance the division of labor within the household. For example, if one partner is exceptionally gifted in at-home repairs or yard work, they might take on those tasks while the other partner focuses on cooking, cleaning, or child care. By sharing responsibilities in this way, both partners can use their natural gifts to contribute meaningfully to the household.

2. Emotional support: Gifting can also support relationship equity by providing emotional support and nurturing. For example, if one partner is exceptionally gifted at listening

and offering guidance, they might provide emotional support for their partner during times of stress or difficulty. Similarly, suppose one partner is gifted at creating a relaxing and comfortable environment. In that case, they might help create a peaceful and supportive home for their partner to return to daily.

3. Personal growth: Finally, gifting can also support each other's personal growth and development. For example, if one partner is gifted at helping others set and achieve goals, they might offer support and guidance as their partner pursues a new career or personal passion. Similarly, one partner is gifted at providing constructive feedback and helping others learn and grow. In that case, they might offer support as their partner develops new skills or works to overcome personal challenges.

Gifting creates a sense of balance and equity within the relationship, with both partners contributing their unique gifts and talents to support each other in meaningful ways. The partners feel valued and appreciated for their unique contributions.

Disadvantages of not promoting the use of natural gifts and talents

1. Unbalanced division of labor: If one partner is not utilizing their natural gifts and talents, the other partner may be taking on disproportionate responsibilities, leading to resentment and burnout.

2. Lack of fulfillment: If partners fail to utilize their natural gifts and talents, they may not feel fulfilled in their roles and the relationship, leading to dissatisfaction and potentially causing them to seek fulfillment elsewhere.

3. Missed growth opportunities: If partners are not encouraged to utilize their natural gifts and talents, they may miss out on opportunities for personal and professional growth, limiting their potential and ultimately impacting their overall well-being.

4. Inequitable power dynamics: If one partner is not encouraged or allowed to utilize their natural gifts and

talents, it can lead to an inequitable distribution of power in the relationship, with one partner holding more control and decision-making power than the other.

5. Missed opportunities for collaboration: When partners are encouraged to utilize their natural gifts and talents, it can create opportunities for collaboration and mutual support, as each partner brings unique strengths to the relationship. Without this, the relationship may lack synergy and may not reach its full potential.

6. Unfulfilled potential: If one partner is not encouraged to use their natural gifts and talents, they may not be able to reach their full potential, which can be a loss for the individual and the relationship as a whole.

7. Limited problem-solving abilities: When both partners are not utilizing their natural gifts and talents, they may have limited problem-solving abilities, as they may need access to the full range of skills and knowledge they could bring.

Advantages of promoting the use of natural gifts and talents

1. Increased fulfillment: When partners can use their natural gifts and talents, they may feel more fulfilled and satisfied in their roles within the relationship. It can lead to a greater sense of purpose and meaning in life.

2. More effective problem-solving: When partners are encouraged to utilize their natural gifts and talents, they will be better equipped to solve problems and handle challenges within the relationship. Ultimately, it can lead to more effective communication and tremendous success in resolving conflicts.

3. Better balance of responsibilities: When each partner can contribute in a way that aligns with their natural gifts and talents, it can create a better balance of responsibilities within the relationship. It can also help reduce resentment or burnout that can arise when one partner feels like they are carrying too much of the load.

4. Increased appreciation for each other: When partners recognize and appreciate each other's unique strengths and contributions, it can lead to a more profound sense of connection and appreciation within the relationship.

5. Improved overall relationship satisfaction: When both partners feel fulfilled and appreciated, it can lead to greater satisfaction and happiness. It helps to create a strong foundation for a long-lasting and healthy partnership.

6. Improved self-awareness: When partners are encouraged to explore and utilize their natural gifts and talents, it can lead to greater self-awareness and personal growth, including building self-confidence and a stronger sense of identity.

7. Enhanced creativity: When partners can bring their unique perspectives and talents to the table, it can lead to greater creativity and innovation within the relationship, helping keep things fresh and exciting.

8. Greater flexibility: When partners are open to utilizing their natural gifts and talents in different ways, it can create a greater sense of flexibility and adaptability within the relationship. Partners will be able to navigate changes or challenges that arise over time.

9. Better work-life balance: When partners can utilize their natural gifts and talents in their work and home lives, it can lead to a better balance of work and personal life. It can also help reduce stress and burnout and create a greater sense of harmony overall.

10. More meaningful connections: When partners can connect over shared passions and interests, it can lead to a deeper and more meaningful connection. Hence, creating a strong foundation for a lasting and fulfilling partnership.

Promoting the use of natural gifts and talents in an equitable relationship can have far-reaching benefits for both partners and the relationship. The partners will be able to create a more dynamic, fulfilling, and mutually supportive relationship where each partner can contribute their unique strengths and skills.

(C) Roles. The essence of a truly harmonious marriage lies in the mutual sharing of responsibilities between husband and wife. It transcends the confines of traditional gender-based roles and calls for considering individual interests, unique gifts, strengths, weaknesses, and constraints when assigning tasks within the household. In many societies, such as certain African cultures, the wife has traditionally been designated the role of caregiver and nurturer. Such a role encompasses caring for the children, attending to their needs, ensuring their cleanliness and well-being, preparing meals, and tending to household chores. However, it is of the utmost importance to recognize that these roles should never be assumed by society or culture, nor should they be imposed upon individuals; rather, they should be a matter of personal preference and choice.

When my wife and I tied the knot, I entered into holy matrimony carrying the age-old notion of traditional gender roles. As the self-proclaimed "man of the house," I naturally assumed the responsibility of assembling and fixing things around our humble abode. Little did I know that I was about to embark on a journey of mishaps and frustrations.

It all started when we purchased an exquisite entertainment table from the esteemed kingdom of IKEA. Now, my dear wife possesses an uncanny interest in and skill for assembling such intricate pieces of furniture. She is like a master craftsman in disguise. I vowed, "I shall assemble this table with my own hands," however, because of my misguided gender roles.

Oh, what a grave mistake I made! With my ego inflated and determination in my heart, I delved into the assembly process. One hour turned into two, then three, until finally, after four long, arduous hours, I emerged from the battlefield of screws and instruction manuals, victorious but battered. My back ached, sweat poured down my brow, and frustration clung to my soul. Did I mention that, with all that hard work, the table could have come out looking better put together? The side of the drawer meant to face inside was turned backward. Meanwhile, had I allowed my wife to take charge, that table would have materialized in all its glory within the blink of an eye and been done perfectly. She possesses an innate ability to piece things together effortlessly without even glancing at the perplexing instructions that confounded me.

Alas, my stubbornness did not end there. In another whimsical tale, we acquired an excellent bicycle for our beloved son, a two-wheeled wonder awaiting its destiny. Once again, my archaic beliefs urged me to seize the task, for assembling a bicycle was undoubtedly a man's duty. I discarded my wife's expertise, dismissing it as inconsequential. How wrong I was!

For two painstaking hours, I grappled with the bolts and gears, fervently following the instructions with unwavering determination. Alas, my efforts were in vain. As I beheld the finished product, the wheels hung in an unbalanced, precarious manner, a testament to my failed endeavor. It dawned upon me then that my insistence on adhering to rigid gender roles punished me with humiliation and endangered my dear son, who may have suffered the perils of an ill-assembled bicycle. And to add salt to the wound, I deprived my wife of her true gift, preventing her from indulging in the joy of exercising her natural talents. It was a disheartening realization that we were missing out on the magnificence of each other's strengths.

Thus, a transformation began to take shape within the recesses of my mind and heart. I learned that true marital bliss lies not in conforming to outdated expectations but in embracing each partner's unique strengths and abilities. I humbly admitted that my wife was the true hero in assembly and fixing. Her skills surpassed my feeble attempts, leaving me in awe and admiration.

Since those fateful events, I have humbly supported her talents, allowing her to flourish in her areas of expertise. Of course, I still lend a helping hand around the house to alleviate her burdens, but I now recognize her as the genuine MVP of assembly. Her ability to mend and construct without instructions astounds me and fills my heart with pride.

Dear reader, let this tale remind us that gender roles can lead us astray, causing more harm than good. Instead, let us celebrate the diverse strengths within the sacred bond of marriage. By embracing and fostering each other's talents, we genuinely unlock the path to harmonious relationships.
The shifting tides of history have had a significant influence on the concept of roles over time. In farming, men were predominantly responsible for working the fields, while women dedicated themselves to the home and children. Women were vital in

Gender roles can lead us astray, causing more harm than good. Instead, let us celebrate the diverse strengths within the sacred bond of marriage.

providing care, crafting clothes, educating their children, nurturing their families, and even bearing children, as Elaine Leeder eloquently states in her book, "The Family in Global Perspective: A Gendered Journey."

The rise of the industrial age, particularly during World War II, brought about a significant shift in women's roles. With many men at war, women were called upon to fill the labor shortage in factories, thereby supporting the war effort and fundamentally transforming their societal roles. Women's contributions strengthened the entire nation and forever altered the fabric of society.

The post-war years marked a profound restructuring of the roles of husbands and wives, as both partners became actively engaged in household chores, childcare, and managing their careers. In the 19th century, the husband or father was predominantly assigned the provider role in the American family. This structure persisted until 1980, when the US Census ceased automatically designating the male as the head of the household. As economic provisions increasingly stemmed from participation in the labor force or commercial ventures, the provider role gained greater significance, while the influence of the housewife role gradually diminished. Work became intertwined with gender identity. Throughout the 20th century, many married women joined the labor force and assumed a share of the provider role.

It is no longer expected in a dual-career family that the woman alone should be responsible for cooking and managing the household. After all, the home belongs to both partners, and duties should be shared to avoid overwhelming one individual. For instance, while one partner cooks, the other may set the table or take charge of dishwashing. This collective effort ensures that all hands are on deck, eliminating the burden of a single person shouldering all household responsibilities.

Cooking, once confined to traditional gender roles, has transcended such limitations. We now witness an increasing number of men embracing their culinary skills and using them to nourish and provide for their families. In cultures like the Samoan culture in Hawaii, the husbands take charge of all cooking duties, challenging the notion that cooking is solely a woman's domain. During a visit to Hawaii, I had the opportunity to immerse myself in their culture and gain a newfound understanding. It became evident to me that what a woman can do, a man can do equally well. Traditionally, the building of the '*umu*', the underground oven, and the cooking of food were tasks carried out by Samoan men, while women assisted by gathering firewood and collecting leaves to cover the rock oven.

In an equitable relationship, both partners should have equal opportunities to participate in and share responsibilities for household tasks, childrearing, and career management. Doing this requires transcending the confines of traditional gender norms and acknowledging and leveraging each partner's unique strengths and preferences.

Examples of equitable roles in a relationship

1. Shared responsibilities: In an equitable relationship, both partners share responsibilities for household tasks. For example, if one partner cooks dinner, the other might wash the dishes or clean the kitchen. Alternatively, if one partner does the laundry, the other partner might vacuum the floors or dust the furniture.

2. Child-rearing: Equitable roles include sharing responsibilities for getting the kids ready for school in the morning, taking turns feeding or bathing the children, or

dividing responsibilities for transporting the children to and from extracurricular activities.

3. Career management: Equitable roles in career management include both partners pursuing their professional goals, with each partner taking turns supporting the other when necessary. For example, if one partner needs to work late, the other partner might handle the evening's household tasks or child-rearing responsibilities.

4. Flexibility: Equitable roles in a relationship mean being flexible and adaptable to changing circumstances. For example, if one partner is sick, the other might take on more household tasks and child-rearing responsibilities. Similarly, if one partner is experiencing a hectic time at work, the other partner might take on more responsibilities at home to support them.

5. Communication: Equitable roles in a relationship involve open and honest communication. For example, partners might discuss their strengths and preferences to determine

how to divide responsibilities. They might also check in with each other regularly to see how the division of labor is working and whether any adjustments are needed.

6. Finances: If one partner is better at managing finances, they might be responsible for paying bills and budgeting, while the other might be responsible for grocery shopping and meal planning. Also, one partner might be good at making money or budgeting money, while the other is good at multiplying the money through various investments.

The key to equitable roles in a marriage is to have open and ongoing communication about each partner's strengths, preferences, and priorities. The partners should have an equal say in decision-making, and each partner's contributions should be recognized and appreciated.

It is also essential to recognize that roles may shift over time, depending on changing circumstances and needs. For example, suppose one partner becomes ill or needs to take a temporary leave from work. In that case, the other partner might need to take on more household tasks and child-rearing responsibilities. There are also seasons where the breadwinner, or the person making the most, no longer does so due to job loss or a career change that might yield a low income at the beginning. More financial responsibilities will fall on the other partner during that season. In an equitable relationship, both partners should be willing to be flexible and adapt as needed to support each other and the family as a whole.

It is also essential to recognize that roles may shift over time, depending on changing circumstances and needs.

Couples face challenges when it comes to practicing equitable roles. Some of the challenges include:

1. Societal expectations and gender roles: Many societies have traditionally assigned specific roles and responsibilities to men and women, making it challenging to practice equitable roles in a relationship.

2. Communication barriers: Couples may need help communicating their needs and expectations around domestic responsibilities, leading to misunderstandings and an unbalanced division of labor.

3. Personal preferences: Couples may have different preferences and strengths regarding domestic tasks, making it challenging to divide responsibilities equitably.

4. Time constraints: Busy work schedules and other responsibilities can make it challenging for both partners to share domestic tasks equally.

5. Resistance to change: Some partners may resist changing their behavior or habits, making shifting to an equitable division of labor challenging.

In order to prevent these challenges and make couples practice equitable roles, it is essential to have open and honest communication about each partner's expectations and preferences. Couples can also benefit from seeking external support, such as counseling, to help them navigate the challenges of practicing equitable roles. Additionally, couples can work together to identify their strengths and weaknesses and create a division of labor that matches their strengths and preferences. Finally, couples need to challenge traditional gender roles and societal expectations and strive toward creating a more equitable and balanced relationship.

Not practicing equitable roles in a relationship can have several disadvantages, including:

1. Resentment: If one partner is responsible for most household tasks and childcare, it can lead to resentment and unfairness. It can create a sense of distance and tension in the relationship.

2. Lack of support: If one partner is focused solely on their career while the other is responsible for most household and childcare tasks, it can create a sense of isolation and a lack of support for the partner taking on most of the domestic responsibilities.

3. Gender role reinforcement: Following traditional gender roles can reinforce outdated and limiting gender stereotypes. It will create a sense of inequality in the relationship and limit each partner's potential and opportunities.
4. Overwork and burnout: If one partner is responsible for most household and childcare tasks, it can lead to overwork and burnout. It can create a sense of exhaustion and stress, which can spill over into other areas of the relationship, such as intimacy.

5. Stifled personal growth: If one partner is responsible for most domestic responsibilities, it can limit their ability to pursue personal growth and development. It can create a sense of stagnation in the relationship and limit each partner's potential.

Overall, not practicing equitable roles in a relationship can lead to unfairness, a lack of support, reinforcement of gender roles, overwork and burnout, and stifled personal growth. Practicing equitable roles can create a sense of balance, support, and shared responsibility in the relationship.

Advantages of practicing equitable roles

1. **Shared responsibility:** When both partners share household and childcare responsibilities, it creates a sense of shared responsibility and accountability. It can create a more balanced and fair relationship.

2. **Reduced stress:** shared domestic responsibilities between partners can reduce stress and workload for each partner. It can create a sense of relaxation and free time, improving overall well-being.

3. **Flexibility:** Having both partners share responsibilities creates a more flexible and adaptable environment. It also creates a sense of spontaneity and openness in the relationship.

4. **Personal growth:** Where both partners share responsibilities, there is space for personal growth and development. Each partner can pursue their interests and passions outside of their domestic responsibilities.

5. **Mutual respect:** When both partners share responsibilities, it creates a sense of mutual respect and appreciation. Each partner's contribution is valued and acknowledged, which can create a sense of gratitude and affection.

Practicing equitable roles in a relationship can create a sense of shared responsibility, reduced stress, flexibility, personal growth, and mutual respect. Ultimately leading to a more balanced, fulfilling, and satisfying relationship for both partners.

(d) Submission. Submission, which is often misunderstood and misrepresented, is far from one-sided. It is a dynamic and nuanced concept intertwined with humility and profound leadership qualities. Consider how Jesus, in his humility, submitted to John the Baptist for baptism, showcasing the essence of submission (Matthew 3:13). Moreover, Jesus exemplified leadership through servitude by humbly washing the feet of his disciples (John 13:14). He even taught his disciples that true greatness is found in being the least and serving others (Luke 22:24–26).

In marriage, the Bible emphasizes mutual submission between husband and wife (Ephesians 5:21). Before wives are encouraged to submit to their husbands (Ephesians 5:22), both partners are told to submit to one another. This mutual submission fosters harmonious cooperation and helps navigate situations where decisions may seem challenging. In such instances, seeking divine guidance and considering each other's perspectives can lead to the best outcomes. Mutual submission should never engender feelings of inferiority; instead, it is a testament to both partners' commitment to the overall success of the relationship.

Submission can positively affect equitable relationships when practiced in consensual, respectful, and balanced ways. It becomes a gesture of trust and respect, acknowledging and appreciating each partner's decision-making abilities. In an equitable relationship, both partners share equal influence and responsibility, ensuring that the outcomes result from shared collaboration and mutual understanding.

...he who is greatest among you, let him be as the younger, and he who governs as he who serves. - Luke 22:26

Here are a few ways that submission can play a role in equitable relationships:

1. **Voluntary submission:** Submission should always be voluntary in an equitable relationship. Both partners should feel comfortable with the idea of submission and agree on how it will be practiced in the relationship.

2. **Respect for boundaries:** Submission, when practiced in an equitable relationship, should be done to respect each partner's boundaries and limits. The partner submitting should feel comfortable communicating their boundaries and limits, and the partner receiving the submission should respect those boundaries.

3. **Active Listening:** Submission involves actively listening to your partner's ideas, concerns, and perspectives without dismissing or invalidating them. It means considering

their thoughts and genuinely seeking to understand their perspectives.

4. **Compromise and Flexibility:** Submission in a relationship often requires finding a middle ground and being open to compromise. It involves being willing to adjust your preferences or plans to accommodate the needs and desires of your partner while also expressing your own needs and boundaries.

5. **Emotional Support:** Submission includes providing emotional support and encouragement to your partner. It means being a source of comfort and strength during challenging times and showing empathy and understanding.

6. **Shared Decision-Making:** Submission does not imply one person making all the decisions or having all the power. Instead, it involves collaborative decision-making where both partners contribute their insights and opinions. It means valuing and incorporating each other's

perspectives to reach mutually beneficial outcomes.

7. **Servant Leadership:** Acts of service and selflessness are ways to demonstrate submission. Both partners can take turns caring for each other's needs, whether taking on household chores, preparing meals, or assisting with personal responsibilities. It involves actively looking for ways to support and uplift each other.

8. **Mutual Trust and Respect:** Submission thrives in an atmosphere of trust and respect. It means valuing your partner's input, trusting their judgment, and respecting their autonomy. It requires treating each other as equals and appreciating each person's unique qualities and strengths in the relationship. The partner submitting should trust the other partner's decision-making abilities, and the partner receiving the submission should respect the other partner's needs and desires.

Submission can play a role in equitable relationships when practiced in a consensual, respectful, and balanced manner. When both partners are comfortable with the idea of submission, which is done in a way that respects each partner's boundaries and equal power balance, it can create a more profound sense of intimacy and trust between partners.

Submission can also be challenging for couples, as it involves giving up some level of control and autonomy in the relationship.

Here are some common challenges couples may face with submission:

1. **Imbalance of power:** When submission is not practiced equitably, it can create an imbalance of power in the relationship. The partner submitting may feel like they have no say in the relationship, while the partner receiving the submission may feel like they have too much power.

2. **Misunderstandings and miscommunication:** Submission can be challenging to understand and communicate effectively. Couples may have different ideas about what submission means and how it should be practiced, leading to misunderstandings and mis-communication.

3. **Conflicts and disagreements:** When one partner submits to the other partner's decisions, conflicts and disagreements may arise if the submitting partner disagrees. It can be challenging to find a way to resolve these conflicts in a way that respects both partners' needs and desires.

4. **Resistance and discomfort:** Some couples may find that submission is uncomfortable or unfamiliar and may resist practicing it in their relationship. It can be challenging to find a way to introduce the concept of submission and make it feel natural and comfortable for both partners.

5. **Personal boundaries:** Submission can involve giving up some personal autonomy, which can be challenging for some individuals who value their independence and autonomy. Couples need to have open and honest communication about personal boundaries and limitations when it comes to submission.

As challenging as submission can be for couples to navigate, it can also be a way to deepen intimacy, trust, and respect in the relationship when practiced in an equitable and consensual manner.

Disadvantages of not practicing submission

1. **Lack of trust:** Submission can be a way to build trust in a relationship, and not practicing it can result in a lack of trust between partners. When one partner feels uncomfortable submitting to the other, it can create a sense of distance and disconnect.

2. **Communication issues:** Submission can also be a way to communicate needs and desires in a relationship. When one partner feels uncomfortable expressing their needs or desires, it can lead to communication issues and misunderstandings.

3. **Power struggles:** Without submission, there can be power struggles in a relationship where each partner vies for control and dominance. It can create a sense of

competition and tension in the relationship.

4. **Lack of intimacy:** Submission can be a way to deepen intimacy and emotional connection in a relationship. Without it, there may be a lack of emotional and physical intimacy between partners.

5. **Inequality:** Inequality in the relationship can be experienced when submission is not equitably practiced. One partner may have more power and control than the other, which can lead to feelings of resentment and unhappiness.

Advantages of practicing submission

1. **Building trust:** Submission can be a way to build trust between partners, as it involves a level of vulnerability and openness. When one partner submits to the other, it can create a sense of safety and security.

2. **Deepening intimacy:** Submission can also be a way to deepen intimacy and emotional connection in a relationship. It can create a sense of closeness and shared

experience between partners.

3. **Enhancing communication:** Submission can be a way to communicate needs and desires in a relationship. When one partner submits to the other, it can create a space for open and honest communication.

4. **Reducing conflict:** When one partner submits to the other, it can reduce conflict. It can create a sense of unity and shared purpose, reducing disagreements and misunderstandings.

5. **Balancing power:** Partners can achieve power balance when submission is equitably practiced. Each partner has a role to play, and each partner's needs and desires are respected and valued.

Practicing submission in a relationship can create a sense of trust, intimacy, communication, and balance. Submission should be practiced equitably and consensually.

(e) Decision-Making. In the realm of decision-making, let harmony be the guiding light. For decisions to be just and proper, let the voices of both parties shine through. Gone are the days of rigid roles where one's domain determined control. Childcare and nourishment were once bestowed on the mother's crest, and finance and business on the father's. Nevertheless, let us transcend these age-old norms and embrace a partnership that reforms. Each choice should be made in an informed manner, where thoughts and dreams are mutually explored.

In the dance of decisions, no one should be left behind. For unity and understanding, we must find them. Disregard not the other's heartfelt plea, for exclusion births discontent and disharmony. It is deemed unfair when a decision is made without considering the other party's idea. It is perceived that the other person is unimportant or that their idea is not valued. It brings unfairness and leads to dissatisfaction in the relationship.

If one holds expertise in a specific field, let them lead with wisdom, acknowledging the bond they wield. If past mistakes in making wrong decisions have caused strife and woe, rebuild trust by ensuring we go down shared paths.

Let every voice resound with grace and care; a husband's leadership role is one to share. Seek counsel from your wife; her wisdom is like a guiding spirit that walks beside you. She offers support and helps chart your course; she is a blessing from above, an ally, and a driving force. As a queen advises the king's noble reign, so does she, the advisor, free from disdain.
Women possess an innate gift so rare: an intuition that transcends all despair. They sense danger lurking from afar, offering caution and protection like a guiding star. Though they may not articulate each detail, heed their warnings, for their insights prevail. By dismissing their voice, you risk defeat, jeopardizing the family you both hold dear.

The Bible calls the woman the helper; it is the same name the Bible calls the Holy Spirit (*English Standard Version Bible*, 2016; John 14:26). That means the wife serves the same role, or we can say she is a mini-Holy Spirit who can help and guide the men. She is the neck that turns the head in the right direction, just like the Holy

Spirit. The wife supports where the man is headed and leads the family. She wants to help the man prosper in business, career, and ministry. Whoever has found a wife obtains favor from the Lord (*English Standard Version Bible*, 2016, Proverbs 18:22) because she is the helper (mini-holy spirit) that helps the man obtain favor from God.

Women possess an innate gift so rare: an intuition that transcends all despair.

The husband should always consult her queen, igniting her inner light. In realms of power, wise rulers heed the advice, consulting their experts, for they hold the prize. Just as managers seek their employees' insight, acknowledging their expertise shines bright. So, the husband should value his wife's grace as the subject matter expert.

By embracing her wisdom, tranquility, and unity, she will take wings—no longer a world where men alone reign but a shared dominion where love shall sustain. Let the decision-making be a tapestry of we, where both husband and wife together decree. Equitable rulership finds its rightful place in the harmonious union of their hearts' embrace.

Challenges Couples Face With Decision-Making:

1. **Unequal power dynamics:** One of the biggest challenges in practicing equitable decision-making is navigating unequal power dynamics within the relationship. For example, if one partner has more financial or social power than the other, ensuring both partners have an equal say in decision-making may take time and effort.

2. **Communication issues:** Another challenge that couples may face is communication issues. Even if both partners are committed to practicing equitable decision-making, they may need help communicating their needs and desires effectively. It can lead to misunderstandings and conflicts, making it challenging to make joint decisions.

3. **Different values and priorities:** Another challenge that couples may face is having different values and priorities.

Even if both partners are committed to equitable decision-making, they may have different ideas about what is most important in their lives. It can make it challenging to make joint decisions that are in the relationship's best interest.

4. **External pressures:** Couples may also face external pressures that make it challenging to practice equitable decision-making. For example, suppose one partner's family has strong opinions or expectations about decisions; navigating those external pressures may be complex while maintaining an equitable relationship.

5. **Personal biases:** Finally, couples may face challenges due to personal biases that they hold. For example, if one partner has internalized societal messages about gender roles, they may struggle to see their partner as equal in decision-making.

While equitable decision-making can be challenging when building a solid and healthy relationship, couples can create a more balanced and fulfilling relationship by being aware of these challenges and working to overcome them.

Ways decision-making can contribute to relationship equity

1. **Equal participation:** In an equitable relationship, both partners should have an equal say in decision-making, regardless of gender or social status. Partners should feel comfortable sharing their opinions and ideas, and both should be willing to listen to and consider each other's perspectives.

2. **Shared decision-making:** Equitable relationships involve shared decision-making where both partners have an equal role. For example, suppose a couple is deciding where to go on vacation. In that case, both partners should have an equal say in the decision, and the final choice should be a compromise that considers both partners' preferences.

3. **Respectful communication:** Equitable decision-making involves respectful communication. Both partners should be willing to communicate honestly and respectfully, and

both should be willing to listen to each other's concerns and needs. Both partners should be willing to compromise and make decisions in the relationship's best interest.

4. **Trust:** Equitable decision-making requires trust between partners. Both partners should trust each other to make decisions that are in the relationship's best interest and be willing to support each other's decisions.

5. **Flexibility:** Equitable decision-making also involves flexibility. Both partners should be willing to adapt and adjust their decisions based on changing circumstances or new information that may arise. Partners should be willing to reconsider their decisions if they are no longer working or if new information comes to light.

Here are some disadvantages to not practicing equitable decision-making:

1. **Resentment and frustration:** When one partner consistently makes all the decisions, it can lead to resentment and frustration in the other partner. Over time,

this can create a power imbalance in the relationship that is difficult to overcome.

2. **Lack of trust:** If one partner consistently makes all the decisions, it can lead to a lack of trust between partners. The partner who feels left out of the decision-making process may begin to feel like their opinions and ideas should be valued and respected.

3. **Unbalanced workload:** When one partner makes all the decisions, it can create an unbalanced workload in the relationship. The partner who is not involved in decision-making may feel like they are doing all the "grunt work" without having a say in the direction of the relationship.

4. **Poor outcomes:** One-sided decision-making can lead to poor outcomes for both partners. The partner making the decisions may need more information or perspectives to make the best decision for the relationship.

5. **Limited personal growth:** When one partner consistently

makes all the decisions, it can limit the personal growth and development of the other partner. The partner who is not involved in decision-making may feel like they are not growing or learning in the relationship.

By working to create a more balanced and equitable decision-making process, couples can build a stronger, more fulfilling relationship that benefits both partners.

Advantages of practicing equitable decision-making in a relationship

1. **Improved communication:** Practicing equitable decision-making requires open and honest communication between partners. Couples can improve their communication skills and better understand each other's needs and perspectives by working together to make joint decisions.

2. **Increased trust:** When both partners have an equal say in decision-making, it can help build trust and mutual respect. It can also lead to more vital intimacy and

connection between partners.

3. **Better outcomes:** Equitable decision-making can lead to better outcomes for both partners. When both partners can provide input and collaborate to make decisions, it can lead to more creative and innovative solutions that benefit everyone involved.

4. **Shared responsibility:** When both partners are involved in decision-making, it creates a sense of shared responsibility for the outcomes. It can lead to a stronger sense of part-nership and collaboration.

5. **Reduced conflict:** When both partners feel heard and respected in decision-making, it can help reduce conflict and disagreements. Also, it can create a more harmonious and peaceful relationship overall.

Overall, decision-making plays a vital role in an equitable relationship because it allows both partners to feel valued and respected and promotes a sense of balance and mutual trust. By making decisions together, both partners can work towards shared goals and create a stronger and more fulfilling relationship.

Chapter Four

Advantages Of Relationship Equity And Disadvantages Of Not Practicing Relationship Equity

Relationship equity is the value and benefits derived from long-term, mutually beneficial relationships between individuals, organizations, or businesses. It is a measure of the strength, trust, and goodwill built over time. Note: I mentioned organizations and businesses, but our focus here is on a man and a woman.

Relationship equity has its advantages, and in this chapter, I will be listing them.

- It helps the spouses unite, have harmony, and operate with one mind. "Do two walk together unless they have agreed to meet?" (*English Standard Version Bible*, 2016; Amos 3:3). God wants us to operate with one mind. When He made Adam, He breathed life into him. When he made Eve, he did not breathe life into her because he wanted them to operate from one mind. In the story of the Tower of Babel, which is the first skyscraper in the world, the people got far because they agreed (*English Standard Version Bible*, 2016; Genesis 11:6).

- It spurs economic growth for the partners. The reward of two people shall be great (*English Standard Version Bible*, 2016, Ecclesiastes 4:9). Another scripture mentions that one shall chase a thousand and two shall chase ten thousand (*English Standard Version Bible*, 2016; Deuteronomy 32:30). God wants us to be fruitful. When we are egalitarian in our practice, we are bound to enjoy the promises of God for our marriage.

- It allows husbands and wives to make the best decisions for their families and does not confine their options to traditional ideologies.

- Women are treated with fairness as opposed to being seen as property. They can pursue their careers, education, personal fulfillment, and opportunities to make a difference in their lives and others.

- It balances the house chores without one person's feelings being burned out.

- Greater satisfaction: Equitable relationships are often more fulfilling for both partners. When each partner feels valued and heard, they are more likely to feel content and happy in the relationship.

- Improved communication: Practicing equity requires open and honest communication, which in turn helps improve communication skills between partners. It can lead to better problem-solving and conflict resolution.

- Improved mental health: Equity in a relationship can reduce stress and anxiety levels and improve mental health outcomes for both partners.

- Stronger connection: When partners feel equally important and invested in the relationship, they are likely to feel a stronger emotional connection.

- Improved intimacy: Practicing equity in a relationship can lead to improved intimacy and sexual satisfaction. Both partners are more likely to feel comfortable and connected when they are respected and heard.

- Better conflict resolution: When both partners have an equal say in decision-making and respect each other's opinions, conflicts can be resolved more effectively and without resentment.

- Shared responsibility: When both partners share the workload and responsibility, it can lead to a sense of teamwork and a stronger bond.

- It breeds trust and loyalty. When individuals have a history of delivering on commitments and values, trust and loyalty are built.

- There is flexibility and adaptability. When parties develop equity in their relationship, they become more flexible in their opinions and adapt to each other. You can blend despite differences in opinion and character. You don't merely tolerate each other; you accept each other.

Building and maintaining relationship equity requires time, effort, and genuine commitment from both parties. It contributes not just to a successful relationship but also to the success and growth of the couples involved. Practicing equity in a relationship can lead to a more fulfilling, satisfying, and healthier partnership for both individuals involved.

We can see a lot of advantages in relationship equity. It will suffice to say that when relationship equity is not practiced, it will be very dangerous for couples. Below is a list of the disadvantages of not practicing relationship equity.

Disadvantages of Not Practicing Relationship Equity

- It can lead to communication breakdowns and, hence, divorce. When one spouse believes in relationship equity and the other person does not, they will be operating on two minds, two visions ("Di" means two in Greek), and if you put the word "Di" in front of "vision," you have division.

- The partners will not be able to maximize their family unit; only some of the resources, gifts, knowledge, and ideas the individuals possess will be utilized to bring results for the family and children.

- It can prevent the under-benefitted person from fulfilling the purpose of God in their lives.

- It will erode love: A partner may feel like they are not loved when their opinion is not heard and considered in decision-making.

- It breeds resentment and dissatisfaction. This happens when one partner consistently feels he or she is carrying an unfair burden or not receiving equal treatment. Over time, this can create a rift between partners and erode the foundations of trust and mutual support.

- Imbalance of responsibilities: Without practicing relationship equity, there is a higher likelihood of an imbalance in the distribution of responsibilities within the marriage. One partner may end up shouldering the majority of household chores, childcare duties, or financial obligations, while the other partner may enjoy a more relaxed or privileged role. This imbalance can lead to feelings of being overwhelmed, taken for granted, or undervalued.

- Emotional disconnection: When one partner consistently feels that their needs, desires, or contributions are not given equal importance, it can result in emotional disconnection. The neglected partner may withdraw emotionally, leading to loneliness and isolation. Over time, this can deteriorate the intimacy and emotional bond between partners.

- Limited personal growth: Relationship equity involves recognizing and supporting each partner's goals, aspirations, and personal growth. When this is lacking, one or both partners may find themselves restricted or hindered in pursuing their interests and personal development. It can lead to stagnation or unfulfilled potential, thereby affecting overall life satisfaction.

- Communication breakdown: It can be challenging for partners to express their concerns, needs, or desires when equity needs to be included, leading to a breakdown in communication and understanding.

- Increased conflict: The lack of relationship equity can increase conflict within the marriage. Resentment, frustration, and unmet expectations can manifest as disagreements, arguments, or passive-aggressive behavior. Over time, unresolved conflicts can create a toxic and hostile environment that further strains the relationship.

- There is a lack of loyalty and trust. This is where cheating comes in. Couples find it difficult to stand and support each other. They can't trust each other, even in the area of finances, and chaos is the order of the day. The other party, who is on the receiving end, feels unfairly treated.

- There is imbalance and inequality. At this point, one of the couples may feel burdened with more responsibilities and efforts while receiving fewer benefits in return.

- Decreased relationship satisfaction. When one of the partners feels he or she is not receiving his or her fair share, there is dissatisfaction in the relationship, which can lead to a decline in the relationship and even a dissolution.

To avoid all these, it is important for individuals in a relationship to actively strive for relationship equity by maintaining open communication, negotiating, compromising, and ensuring fairness in the distribution of responsibilities and benefits.

Chapter Five

Building A Lasting And Fulfilling Partnership

"Fairness, Respect, and Love: The Secrets to a Successful Equity-Based Relationship!"

As someone who values strong and harmonious relationships, I'd like to share some thoughts and advice with you about the significance of relationship equity and its role in cultivating a long-lasting and fulfilling partnership. A successful and long-lasting relationship is built on fairness, support, and mutual understanding. This is where the pillars of successful relationship-building come into play. These pillars serve as guiding principles that can help you and your partner develop a strong and balanced partnership that can withstand the challenges and tests of time.

Using the concept of equity to build a successful relationship entails developing and sustaining a strong foundation of justice, equality, and mutual respect. It goes beyond traditional conceptions of balance, aiming for an inclusive and just collaboration that recognizes and tackles power dynamics, privileges, and inequities.

A successful equity-based partnership necessitates open and honest communication.

To begin, developing a successful equity-based partnership necessitates open and honest communication. Both partners should feel free to express their wants, desires, and concerns without fear of being judged or retaliated against. Active listening and empathy are critical to understanding each other's points of view and experiences, enabling meaningful discourse and problem-solving. Equity also entails recognizing and removing any existing biases or preconceptions that may impede the partnership. Individuals must commit to self-reflection and ongoing learning to understand and fight their privilege, unconscious biases, and systemic impediments that might perpetuate injustice. Partners may build a more equal and inclusive environment for each other by actively trying to remove these barriers.

Another crucial part of leveraging equity to develop a successful relationship is the equitable sharing of tasks and decision-making. Both couples should have an equal say in important decisions, rather than one person dominating them. Recognizing and appreciating each other's efforts, whether financial, emotional, or domestic, is critical for instilling a sense of fairness and shared responsibility. Furthermore, adopting equity to develop a healthy partnership necessitates recognizing and correcting power disparities. This entails investigating potential dynamics depending on gender, race, financial background, or other types of identity. Partners should actively fight to dismantle oppressive institutions and create an atmosphere where both individuals may thrive. Empathy and understanding are essential for a fair connection. It entails acknowledging and validating each other's experiences, emotions, and points of view. This offers a secure and supportive environment where both partners can be vulnerable, communicate their needs, and receive the support they need to grow and develop. Developing a successful equality-based relationship requires a consistent commitment to growth, understanding, and fairness. It entails questioning society's standards and actively attempting to build an inclusive partnership that equally honors and respects both members. Partners who embrace equity principles can create a strong and lasting partnership based on trust, respect, and similar ideals.

1. **A FAIR DISTRIBUTION OF RESPONSIBILITIES:** This is the first tool for an effective partnership. The equitable distribution of responsibilities is one of the key factors that contribute to a healthy and thriving relationship. It emphasizes the importance of fair and balanced task sharing within and outside the household. It creates a sense of equality and prevents one partner from shouldering most of the workload when responsibilities are divided based on individual strengths, interests, and availability. In our church, my wife serves in the protocol department, so she works with

the pastor, and after the church service, I do wait for her. However, when we started having children, instead of waiting for my wife, I would take the children home, fix their meals, bathe them, tuck them into bed, and prepare them for school the next day. This way, I share domestic responsibility with my wife by not waiting for her to come home and do all that, and when she comes home, she might even be too tired to do anything. So, I have lifted that burden off her shoulders. A fair distribution of responsibilities between couples is crucial for maintaining balance, harmony, and equity in the relationship. Here are a few things to think about when it comes to the equitable distribution of responsibilities:

- ***Identify Individual Strengths*:** Each partner brings to the relationship unique skills, abilities, and strengths. You can assign tasks that match each person's capabilities by recognizing and leveraging their strengths. For example, if one partner excels in finances, they may take the lead in managing the household budget while the other excels in cooking and meal preparation. Responsibility is distributed in this way based on what each person is naturally good at, making task division more efficient and balanced. For instance, I make money, and my wife also makes money, but my wife knows better how to manage money. Gender roles have to be overlooked when it comes to managing money. As a good coordinator, my wife knows what to pay for, when to pay, and whom to pay. My wife's skill as a coordinator helps her manage the budget. Nevertheless, I am good at multiplying money. After I became an entrepreneur, I had a large sum of money, and my wife suggested we use the money on an investment. I listened to her, looked for an investment opportunity, and we had a 60% return on that money.

- ***Consider Interests and Preferences:*** When assigning responsibilities, it is critical to consider the interests and preferences of both partners. You can create a more satisfying division of responsibilities by involving each other in decision-making and considering what tasks bring joy and fulfillment. This helps to ensure that both partners are engaged and motivated to contribute to the success of the relationship. Work, personal commitments, and other obligations may differ between partners, so balance availability and workload. When assigning respon-sibilities, it is critical to consider each person's availability. It may be reasonable to adjust the distribution of tasks if one partner has a demanding work schedule while the other has more flexibility. Flexibility and understanding in accommodating each other's availability can help achieve a more balanced and equitable division of responsibilities. When both partners are mindful of each other's interests and preferences, it promotes unde-rstanding, respect, and overall satisfaction. You can understand each other when you regularly share your thoughts, desires, and aspirations. There will always be times when your partner's interests and preferences will take precedence, and this is where selflessness and flexibility come in because you have to set your interests aside and support your partner. A healthy relationship involves give and take, understanding, and compromise. By considering each other's interests and preferences, you create an environment where both partners feel valued and supported, leading to a stronger and more fulfilling relationship.

It is crucial to understand that both partners are responsible for each other. Both partners should take an active role in understanding and meeting each other's needs. Let's get back to the case of cooking. I am doing this because cooking can be tedious at times. You realize your wife wants to cook rice and plantains, and you look for ways to help her. This could be by helping with the ingredients, bathing the children, or washing the dishes after the meal. Look for a way to ease the stress on your partner.

2. ***RE-ASSESS AND COMMUNICATE REGULARLY:*** As life circumstances change, it's critical to reassess and adjust the distribution of responsibilities. Communication between partners must be open and honest for both parties to feel heard and understood. Check-in regularly to discuss how the task division works and if any adjustments are required. This ongoing dialogue promotes fairness and prevents resentment or imbalance from developing. Remember that fair responsibility distribution aims to create a partnership in which both individuals feel valued, respected, and supported. It is not necessary to aim for an

exact 50/50 task split (the relationship is 100/100), but rather a balance that reflects the unique dynamics and circumstances of your relationship. Flexibility, comprehension, and effective communication are essential for achieving this balance.

- **Communication that is both open and effective**: Maintain open lines of communication by creating an atmosphere in which both partners feel comfortable expressing their needs, concerns, and desires. Active listening and empathy are essential components of effective communication because they allow you to understand each other's points of view and work together to find mutually beneficial solutions. I'd like to go over this in greater detail.

- Communication is the lifeblood of any happy, healthy relationship. It serves as a foundation for comprehension, connection, and conflict resolution. The "open and effective communication" pillar emphasizes the importance of keeping lines of communication open with your partner. Here's an explanation of what this means and how it can help your relationship:

- Create a non-judgmental environment: It is critical for effective communication to create a safe and non-judgmental environment. Both partners should feel free to express their needs, concerns, and desires without fear of being judged or retaliated against. This entails actively listening to one another, displaying empathy, and not interrupting or dismissing one another's thoughts and feelings. It fosters a deeper sense of emotional intimacy and strengthens the bond between partners when both individuals feel heard and respected.

- Active Listening Should Be Practiced: Active listening entails fully participating in the conversation and giving your full attention to your partner. It entails paying attention not only to the words spoken but also to the underlying emotions and concerns. When your partner is speaking, concentrate on understanding their point of view rather than formulating your response. Check your understanding of what you've heard and express genuine interest in their thoughts and feelings. Active listening fosters a sense of validation and improves understanding between partners. Couples must encourage each other to express their emotions, concerns, and needs openly and without judgment. Actively listen to each other and try to understand each other's perspectives.

3. DEVELOP EMPATHY AND UNDERSTANDING

Empathy is the ability to put yourself in the shoes of your partner and understand their emotions and experiences. Empathy can help you gain a better understanding of each other's points of view and foster compassion and support. Recognize and validate your partner's feelings, even if you don't entirely agree with them. Avoid passing judgment and seek to understand the reasons for their thoughts and emotions. Empathy fosters trust and strengthens the emotional bond in a relationship. Empathy and understanding contribute to emotional connection, effective communication, and relationship satisfaction. When you empathize, you can share mutual feelings and understanding. With empathy, you are attuned to your partner's non-verbal cues as you demonstrate care and support. With this, you can create a safe and supportive environment where your partner feels understood and validated. Understanding in a relationship goes beyond comprehending your partner's emotions; it also encompasses grasping your partner's needs, values, and motivations. This involves open-mindedness and the willingness to see things from your partner's point of view, even if it differs from your own. It also involves acknowledging and respecting their individuality, experiences, and personal growth. With this, you two have an emotional connection, as it allows you to be vulnerable with each other. Empathy and understanding promote open and honest dialogue, and you can avoid misunderstandings and resolve conflicts. You can create a loving and compassionate bond with your partner by cultivating empathy and understanding in your relationship.

4. SEEK MUTUALLY BENEFICIAL SOLUTIONS

Finding mutually beneficial solutions to conflicts and challenges is important to effective communication. When discussing disagreements or making decisions, keep a collaborative mindset in mind. Instead of focusing on who is correct or incorrect, try to find compromises or solutions that meet the needs of both partners. Remember that the goal is to work as a team to help each other grow and be happy.

- Check in regularly and provide feedback. Communication is a continuous process, not a one-time event. Make it a habit to check in with each other regularly, discussing how you're feeling, what's working well, and areas that could use improvement. Constructive feedback delivered lovingly and respectfully assists both partners in understanding each other's expectations and working toward a more fulfilling relationship.

- You can strengthen your emotional connection, foster understanding, and navigate challenges more easily if you prioritize open and effective communication in your relationship. Remember that communication takes effort on the part of both partners, so make a conscious decision to actively listen, empathize, and express yourself honestly and respectfully.

5. MAKE DECISIONS TOGETHER:

Both partners should be involved in decision-making and strive for agreement. Each individual should have an equal voice and be able to contribute their ideas and opinions without fear of being judged. By embracing shared decision-making, you respect each other's autonomy and ensure that important decisions are made collaboratively. This pillar emphasizes the importance of involving both partners in the decision-making process and attempting to reach a consensus. Shared decision-making ensures that both partners have an equal voice in the relationship and are actively involved in making important decisions. It recognizes the worth of each individual's ideas, opinions, and perspectives. Giving equal weight to both partners' contributions fosters respect and equality. Shared decision-making encourages a collaborative approach to decision-making. Instead of one partner making decisions unilaterally or dominating the decision-making process, both partners actively collaborate to find solutions that meet their individual needs and shared goals. This collaborative approach fosters a sense of partnership and teamwork, which helps to strengthen the bond between partners. You can maintain a healthy and successful relationship when you make decisions together because it builds trust and strengthens their bond. Both partners can express their thoughts, concerns, and preferences openly, allowing a deeper understanding of each other's perspectives. Here, active listening is important because it demonstrates respect and validates each partner's input. Couples have a common understanding of what they want to achieve, and when faced with choices, they can sit together and evaluate based on their shared goals and values.

How shared decision-making helps both partners

- ***Autonomy*** and individuality are respected in a healthy relationship. Shared decision-making recognizes and honors this autonomy by allowing both partners to express their thoughts and opinions without fear of judgment or criticism. It recognizes that decisions affecting the relationship should be made jointly, considering both individuals' desires and aspirations.

- ***It breeds consensus.*** The goal of collaborative decision-making is to reach a consensus or agreement that meets the needs of both partners. Active communication, listening, and a willingness to find common ground are all required. It may necessitate compromise, flexibility, and an openness to different points of view. Working toward agreement creates an environment where both partners feel valued, heard, and invested in the decisions shaping their relationship. When there is a consensus, no one feels cheated, and each person's opinion is weighed and considered; no one is over-benefitting, and no one is under-benefitting. Achieving consensus requires effective communication, active listening, empathy, and compromise. Finding a middle ground or alternative solutions when making decisions helps couples accommodate each other's needs and can lead to a mutually satisfying outcome. A healthy consensus is based on equality, where both partners have an equal voice and respect each other's opinions, values, and boundaries. However, consensus may not always be achieved immediately, as it may take time to work through differences and find solutions that satisfy both partners. In this case, patience is the key to allowing the process to unfold without rushing or pressuring each other. So, sometimes, it doesn't mean couples will have to agree on everything all the time, but they need to find common ground to make decisions that respect their needs and well-being.

- ***It fosters transparency and honesty.*** Open and honest communication is essential for shared decision-making. Both partners should feel at ease expressing their thoughts, concerns, and preferences. It necessitates a dedication to openness and a willingness to share information that may be relevant to the decision at hand. Transparency and honesty foster trust and strengthen your relationship's foundation.

By embracing shared decision-making, you create a partnership that values both partners' input and contributions. It promotes fairness, respect, and equality in your relationship. Remember that shared decision-making is a continuous process that necessitates active participation and a commitment to open communication. It may not always be easy, and disagreements may arise, but by working together, you can navigate obstacles and make decisions that benefit both partners' well-being and happiness. As a result of shared decision-making in our marriage, my wife and I, with all the money we made over the years, were able to build a multimillion-dollar house sitting on close to six acres of land; that house is our dream house. So, you can be a breadwinner but not always make the decision alone. Making a decision with your partner allows you to think properly and arrive at a consensus that favors you both. Make sure you hear each other's voices in your decision-making.

6. **ENCOURAGEMENT AND ASSISTANCE:** Support and encourage your partner's goals, dreams, and aspirations without fail. Celebrate each other's accomplishments and offer support during difficult times. By cultivating a supportive environment, you lay a solid foundation for personal growth and shared accomplishments.

Here's an explanation of what it means to provide unwavering support and encouragement for your partner's goals, dreams, and aspirations and how it can help your relationship:

⊙ ***Believe in each other***: To support and encourage your partner, you must have complete faith in their abilities and potential. It entails being their cheerleader, championing their goals, and providing reassurance during difficult times.

When you believe in your partner, you give them the confidence and motivation they need to achieve their objectives. When I traveled to Mexico to surprise my wife, who was coordinating a birthday party for a client, I went there to cheer her up. People around me said my presence made a difference because she had been stressed out. You see, I believe in what she is doing. I appreciated what she was doing; all I could do was encourage her and cheer her up.

- ***Celebrate each other's successes.*** Celebrating each other's successes, no matter how big or small, is an important part of mutual support and encouragement. You create a positive and uplifting environment in your relationship by acknowledging and celebrating achievements together. Celebrating each other's successes also reinforces that you are each other's biggest fans and genuinely care about each other's happiness.

- ***Offer assistance.*** Help goes beyond encouraging words. It also entails offering assistance and being present for your partner during difficult times. Your presence and willingness to help can make a significant difference in your partner's journey, whether it's lending a listening ear, providing practical assistance, or simply being a source of emotional support. As a man, if you know your wife is not so good at cooking, you can help her. This may raise some eyebrows in some cultures because of the belief that cooking is strictly for women and that men have no business with cooking. So many marriages have been destroyed because of this. Cooking should not be an issue in marriage if you want to keep your home. Some women were raised in homes where they had cooks and were not allowed to enter the kitchen. They grow up and get married, and it becomes a problem. You will be surprised that some ladies even have an aversion to cooking! Shocking right? And this is where you come in if you love your wife. You can help her. You can both be in the kitchen to do the cooking together if she can cook but hates it, which will encourage her. You can help your wife by teaching her how to cook. Your encouragement and gentleness with her will go a long way. I know of a family where the husband cooks; cooking is no big deal to him. The man is a chef as well. They are not defining gender roles in the family. In another family, the man is a stay-at-home dad. He is always with the children; he plays with them and helps them with their assignments while the wife is making money. The understanding is there, and they can balance. This man has great skills in managing children; he knows how to cheer them up, he is gentle with them, and he understands their emotions. The wife, on the other hand, doesn't have that much patience, so she focuses on her strengths, which are making money and sacrificing for the family, while the husband's strengths are managing the home front. By doing so, they work together harmoniously.

- ***Create a safe space.*** To provide support and encourage-ment, you must first create a safe space where your partner feels comfortable sharing their hopes, fears, and vulnerabilities. It entails not passing judgment and actively listening when they open up to you. You foster a deep sense of trust and intimacy in your relationship by creating this safe space.

7. ***MUTUAL GROWTH AND ACCOMPLISHMENTS:*** When partners support and encourage each other, the groundwork is laid for mutual growth and shared accomplishments. You create an environment where personal growth is valued and celebrated by nurturing each other's goals and aspirations. Your collective accomplishments serve as evidence of your relationship's strength and support. For mutual growth to occur, there must have been self-growth on the part of each partner. When you can work on yourselves, you can help each other.

Remember that encouragement and support are ongoing practices that necessitate consistency and genuine concern for your partner's well-being. By embracing this pillar, you strengthen your bond and foster a nurturing environment for personal and shared success.

8. EMOTIONAL LABOR FAIRNESS: Recognize and address the emotional labor required to maintain a healthy relationship. Emotional labor includes the efforts made to manage and understand one another's emotions, to support one another during difficult times, and to be emotionally present. To avoid emotional exhaustion and resentment, ensure this labor is distributed fairly.

"Fairness in Emotional Labor" emphasizes recognizing and addressing the emotional labor involved in maintaining a healthy and fulfilling relationship.

- Emotional labor is the effort and energy invested in managing and understanding each other's emotions, providing support during difficult times, and being emotionally present in the relationship. It entails being aware of your partner's needs, actively listening, expressing empathy, and creating a safe space for emotional expression.

- ***Emotional support and validation:*** Being fair in emotional labor entails providing your partner with emotional support and validation. During difficult times, be there for one another by lending a listening ear, a comforting presence, and words of encouragement. Validate your partner's emotions by letting them know that you understand and respect their feelings. You need to understand your partner's emotions. Some people are very emotional, and things get at them easily. When a partner makes a mistake that affects him or her, it is not the time to play the blame game. What I mean by the blame game is when you use the sentence "I told you so" in a harsh way. It is time to be there for your partner. The mistake has been made quite well, but you must make amends and find a solution. This helps you both form a stronger bond. But if you keep pointing accusing fingers, your partner could feel dejected. This could be dangerous, as some could get depressed while others could be suicidal. But when you come together to make amends for a mistake committed by a partner, it paves the way for you both to move forward.

- ***Prevent emotional exhaustion and resentment:*** An unequal distribution of emotional labor in a relationship can lead to emotional exhaustion and resentment. We must be aware of each other's emotional well-being and actively work to prevent negative emotions. Check-in with each other regularly to assess the balance of emotional labor and make adjustments as needed. Your partner can come home with only 20% energy after a long work day, and you, on the other hand, may have 80%. In a truly equitable partnership, you can collectively carry each other's percentages to 100%.

If both of you are below 100%, it's important to communicate and find solutions that don't harm each other. This may involve taking time alone to cool off, having intimate moments to alleviate stress, going on a date together, or planning a vacation. The key is to work together without hurting each other through words or actions. You can create an environment where both partners feel valued, supported, and understood by promoting fairness in emotional labor. This equilibrium prevents emotional exhaustion and promotes a more profound connection in your relationship.

Remember that emotional labor fairness is an ongoing process that requires mutual understanding, empathy, and active participation from both partners. By emphasizing this idea, you are laying the groundwork for a relationship that thrives on emotional well-being and mutual support.

You and your partner can cultivate a relationship based on trust, fairness, and mutual respect by implementing the various points stated of building a successful relationship. It is critical to remember that implementing these principles necessitates ongoing commitment and effort on the part of both individuals.

Reflect on these pillars as you embark on this journey together and discuss how you can incorporate them into your relationship.

Understand that there is no gender role. Who gets to do what is not based on gender. The only thing I know that a man cannot do is get pregnant. Men and women are equal, but their strengths are based on their abilities. When you are aware of each other's abilities, you can come to a mutual understanding of what roles to play to help ignite the flame of love in your relationship. The ship you are on together should help you relate well and not find unnecessary faults. When you concentrate on each other's faults, you will never move forward but remain stagnant and frustrated. A home is a place you go to after a day's work to rest, but you cannot find that rest when there is chaos in your home. You should build yourself up to the point where your partner knows he or she is safe with you. Don't be a monster. We are not perfect, but we can work on that level ground where our imperfections are worked on. Reassess your progress regularly and make adjustments as needed. Remember that a healthy and balanced partnership is a work in progress.

I wish you and your partner a lifetime of love, happiness, and peace. May all the principles of successful relationship building, guide you to a fulfilling and lasting bond.

Chapter Six

Relationship Equity Survey

As part of the plan for writing this book, I conducted an online survey asking 50 couples a series of questions to explore whether they practice relationship equity in all five pillars. The majority of the participants (95.5%) identified as black or African American, while the remaining couples consisted of white (4.5%) and Asian individuals (2.3%). The survey had an equal representation of responses from women and men, ensuring a fair balance of gender perspectives. On average, the couples lived together (whether married or in committed relationships) for approximately 13.5 years. The survey responses included options such as agree, strongly agree, disagree, strongly disagree, and neither agree nor disagree.

Power balance: When asked about having an equal voice in their relationship, 46% strongly agreed that they have an equal say, while 40% agreed.

Gifting: In terms of allowing each other to utilize their gifts and talents at home and in other areas of life, most couples (58%) strongly agreed that they support and enable each other to use their strengths.

Roles: Regarding financial management, 50% of couples strongly agreed that they share finances fairly, with minimal arguments about money. Instead of considering gender, the decision about who is in charge of the finances is based on financial expertise, responsibility, and sound money management skills.

When asked about sharing domestic chores moderately, 46% of the participants agreed that they divided chores fairly, while 24% disagreed. Additionally, 52% of the participants agreed that chore allocation is based on personal interest, knowledge, and constraints rather than being dictated by gender. Overall, 50% strongly agreed that they work well together in managing household tasks.

Submission: Regarding submission, 52% of the couples agreed to submit to each other. Participants were also asked about sexual submission and whether they use it as a weapon to deny each other's needs. 48% of respondents agreed that they do not deny each other sex, while only 10% strongly disagreed, indicating instances of sexual denial in their relationships.

Decision Making: The findings revealed that 48% of participants make decisions together on most matters, while only a tiny percentage (10%) disagree that they make joint decisions. Additionally, 50% strongly agreed that they actively listen to each other's viewpoints.

The partners were asked if they were happy and satisfied in their relationship; 58% of participants reported being happy and satisfied, with the same percentage stating that their relationships were healthy.

The survey results show that these couples prioritize equity in their relationship. This commitment to fairness fosters a sense of mutual respect, understanding, and cooperation. As a result, these couples enjoy greater satisfaction, happiness, and overall relationship well-being. The findings of this survey highlight the importance of relationship equity and its positive impact on couples' lives.

Conclusion

The practice of equity and fairness in the workplace is the subject of ongoing debate and even legislation (Cech et al., 2020; McCandless, 2022). However, there is little debate about equity and fairness in romantic relationships outside of feminist rhetoric (Storozhuk & Hoyan, 2018). Fairness and equity are easily detected in business relationships due to clear benchmarks of labor costs, profit, loss, and the exchange of money for goods and services. The legal marriage contract specifies a joint venture in which two individuals cooperatively decide to share their lives, labor, and material goods.

When understood from a romantic perspective, marriage is not a transactional relationship. However, for many years, it has been widely observed that women are marginalized in romantic relationships. Traditionally, men hunted and labored for money while women remained at home with few legal rights to control money or property. This dependent position left women vulnerable to social ills such as child marriage and domestic abuse (Leite et al., 2019). Current roles and expectations have become convoluted as women gain financial independence and contribute to growing equality with men. The relationship becomes more of a power struggle and a source of confusion for the men. The practice of relationship equity eradicates this problem.

Relationship equity theory suggests that relationships can thrive when both partners cooperate with consideration for fairness, strike a balance of power, and everyone uses their gifts to advance the family and personal lives without being restricted due to gender. Fairness can be achieved when people feel they get what they deserve from a relationship.

Relationship equity is a crucial aspect of any healthy, fulfilling partnership. By actively working to create a balance of power, honoring each other's natural gifts and talents, sharing decision-making responsibilities, embracing equitable roles, and approaching submission with mutual respect, couples can cultivate a strong foundation of trust and mutual understanding. The couples will experience a more satisfying, harmonious, and fulfilling relationship.

It is essential to acknowledge that creating and maintaining an equitable relationship requires ongoing effort and commitment from both partners. It is not a one-time fix but a process that requires consistent attention and communication. It may involve identifying areas where one partner may be dominating decision-making or not fully sharing household tasks and actively working to address those imbalances. It may involve re-evaluating traditional gender roles and embracing a more fluid approach that allows both partners to contribute meaningfully.

Furthermore, cultural and societal factors can sometimes make it difficult for couples to practice relationship equity. For example, deeply ingrained gender roles or expectations around submission may be challenging. However, by approaching these challenges with open communication and a willingness to learn and grow, couples can work to create a relationship that is equitable and fulfilling for both partners.

The benefits of practicing relationship equity are numerous. Partners committed to building equity in their relationship experience greater satisfaction, communication, and connection. They are likelier to work collaboratively to overcome challenges and conflicts and are less likely to experience resentment or burnout. In addition, when both partners feel valued and respected, it fosters a sense of intimacy and trust, creating a deeper emotional bond between them.

Life can be better with relationship equity. Empowering the partner spurs economic and development goals for the family. A woman's place should no longer be restricted to the home if she chooses not to. Taking care of the children should not be her job alone. After all, she is not the only one who made the baby. In most societies, standard maternity leave is available for women after having a baby. However, fathers are not given paternity leave. They are expected to use their annual or sick leave. This act suggests that society automatically places the responsibility of raising children primarily on women. It should be the job of both parents. Yes, the baby needs the mother more for food because of the mother's inherited gift that characterizes her as a mother. However, the father still has other roles, such as changing diapers, washing baby bottles, providing food for the wife, giving her emotional support, rocking the baby to sleep, and so many more.

Some people still believe men should only be financial providers and women should be nurturers, restricting them from exploring all the gifts and talents God has given them. Just like men are gifted, God also endows women with so many ideas that have not seen the light of day because men are not comfortable with women who are in powerful positions. Proverbs 31 describes an excellent wife managing the home, caring for children, cooking for her family, and still having her business. She could handle business, the bedroom, and the boardroom.

A real man should not have to restrict his wife from growing, working, developing, attaining higher education, and being all she can be. If a man is confident in himself and his accomplishments, he shouldn't feel intimidated by a woman's success. The best marriages include two flourishing people working together in harmony and enjoying their marriage. An ideal relationship is one in which the husband is 100% himself and the wife is 100% herself. Everyone in the relationship should be able to operate from their rightful position, including their gifts, without experiencing unfairness or inequity.

If the partners have dual-career families, they have the potential to earn more money. They will have more to do with their money. There can be investments they can afford together, and the quality of education for the children will increase, including their standard of living. The couples could also afford to go on family trips and have money saved for the children's future. It does not mean they should only be concerned about money; it is also essential to find a balance to spend time with each other and the children. Until there is gender equity in the relationship, the partners may be unable to maximize the family unit. They will miss out if they put each other in a box and do not maximize their potential. Two are better than one. The power of two creates a marriage. Furthermore, a good leader empowers everyone without suppressing anyone.

Celebrate National Relationship Equity Day (June 24th) With Us

I have created a national day around relationship equity called National Relationship Equity Day. On the beautiful day of June 24th, people worldwide unite to honor and promote the cherished concept of relationship equity every year. Join us in spreading this heartwarming message of harmony across the globe, blending romance and professionalism in perfect harmony.

Here is how to partake in the magic of National Relationship Equity Day:

1. Plan an enchanting date night. Immerse yourselves in the splendor of your town, hand-in-hand. Delight in an exquisite dinner at your favorite restaurant, indulge in a rejuvenating couple's massage, or retreat to a cozy bed and breakfast for a night of pure bliss.

2. Express heartfelt appreciation: Take a tender moment to reflect and compile a list of the gifts, knowledge, and experiences each of you brings to nurture and elevate your relationship. Celebrate the unique contributions you both offer to create a profound bond.

3. Unleash hidden talents and passions. Unleash your imagination together! Create a shared list of untapped gifts or interests waiting to be explored. Discuss the uncharted territories you would have loved to venture into, enhancing your family unit and your personal achievements.

4. Connect with us on Facebook and Instagram.

   Stay updated and be a part of our beloved community by following our page on Facebook and Instagram @Nationalrelationshipequityday

5. Share your love with the world. Who can resist the allure of a captivating love story? Embrace the joy of National Relationship Equity Day by sharing your heartwarming love (in a minute-to-two minutes video or just a picture of you and your partner) on how you practice relationship equity in your marriage. Share this moment on social media platforms like Instagram and Facebook. Tag us and use the hashtag #NationalRelationshipEquityDay.

6. Let us add an element of selfless love to this extraordinary celebration. On this remarkable day, take it upon yourself to alleviate a responsibility that your beloved has carried for too long, granting them a well-deserved respite.

7. Show your support for National Relationship Equity Day by purchasing our exclusive commemorative shirt. With every purchase and proudly displaying it on National Relationship Equity Day, you become an advocate for equitable relationships and contribute to a cause that fosters understanding, harmony, and balance in love.

You can purchase at:

www.relationshipshirt.myshopify.com

Read more about the day at:

www.nationalrelationshipequityday.org

References

1. Hatfield E, Rapson RL, Aumer-Ryan K. Social justice in love relationships: Recent developments. *Social Justice Research.* 2008; 21:413–431.
2. *English Standard Version Bible*, 2016. ESV Online. https://www.biblegateway.com/passage/?search=Ephesians+5%3A23&version=ESV
3. Utne, M. K., Hatfield, E., Traupmann, J., & Greenberger, D. (1984). Equity, marital satisfaction, and stability. Journal of Social and Personal Relationships, 1, 323-332.
4. Stafford, L., & Canary, DJ. (2006). Equity and interdependence as predictors of relational maintenance strategies. *The Journal of Family Communication,* 6(4), 227-254.
5. DeMaris A. The role of relationship inequity in marital disruption. *Journal of Social and Personal Relationships.*

2007;24:177–195.

6. Frisco ML, Williams K. Perceived housework equity, marital happiness, and divorce in dual-earner households. *Journal of Family Issues*. 2003;24:51–73.
7. Joyner K. Justice and the fate of married and cohabiting couples. *Social Psychology Quarterly*. 2009;72:61–76.
8. Gager CT, Sanchez L. Two as one? Couples' perceptions of time spent together, marital quality, and the risk of divorce. *Journal of Family Issues*. 2003;24:21–50.
9. Simon, M. K., & Goes, J. (2013). Assumptions, limitations, delimitations, and scope of the study. https://www.dissertationrecipes.com/wp-content/uploads/2011/04/Assumptions-Limitations-Delimitations-and-Scope-of-the-Study.pdf
10. Xu, Y., Burleson, B. R. (2004). The association of experienced spousal support with marital satisfaction: Evaluating the moderating effects of sex, ethnic culture, and type of support. *Journal of Family Communication*, 4, 123-145.
11. Rabin, C. (1996). *Equal partners—Good friends:*

Empowering couples through therapy. Rutledge.

12. Rabin, C., & Shapira-Berman, O. (1998). Egalitarianism and marital happiness: Israeli wives and husbands on a collision course? *American Journal of Family Therapy, 25*, 319–330.
13. Vanyperen, N. W., & Buunk, B. P. (1990). A longitudinal study of equity and satisfaction in intimate relationships. *European Journal of Social Psychology, 20*, 287–309.
14. Grote, N. K., & Clark, M.S. (2001). Perceiving unfairness in the family: Cause or consequence of marital distress? *Journal of Personality and Social Psychology*, 80, 281—293.
15. Lively, KJ, Steelman, LC, Powell, B (2010) Equity, emotion, and household division of labor. *Social Psychology Quarterly 73*(4), 358–379.
16. Ruppanner, L., Brandén, M., & Turunen, J. (2018). Does unequal housework lead to divorce? Evidence from Sweden. *Sociology*, *52*(1), 75–94.
17. Bernhardt, E, Noack, T, Lyngstad, TH (2008) Shared housework in Norway and Sweden: Advancing the gender

revolution. Journal of European Social Policy 18(3): 275–288.

18. Evertsson, M, Nermo, M (2004) Dependence within families and the division of labor: Comparing Sweden and the United States. Journal of Marriage and Family 66(5): 1272–1286.

19. Fuwa, M (2004) Macro-level gender inequality and the division of household labor in 22 countries. American Sociological Review 69(6): 751–767.

20. Geist, C (2005) The welfare state and the home: Regime differences in the domestic division of labor. European Sociological Review 21(1): 23–41.

21. Oláh, LS, Gähler, M (2014) Gender equality perceptions, division of paid and unpaid work, and partnership dissolution in Sweden. Social Forces 93(2): 571–594.

22. Mckinsey & Company. "Women in the Workplace 2020," September 30, 2020. Retrieved from https://www.mckinsey.com/featured-insights/diversity-and-inclusion/seven-charts-that-show-covid-19s-impact-on-womens-employment

23. Steil, J. M., Weltman, K. Marital inequality: The importance of resources, personal attributes, and social norms on career valuing and the allocation of domestic responsibilities. *Sex Roles* 24, 161–179 (1991).

24. Blom, N., Kraaykamp, G., Verbakel, E. (2017). Couples' division of employment and household chores and relationship satisfaction: A test of the specialization and equity hypotheses. European Sociological Review, 33(2), 195–208.

25. Lively, KJ, Powell, B, Geist, C. (2008) Inequity among intimates: Applying equity theory to the family. Advances in Group Processes 25: 87–115.

26. Lachance-Grzela, M, Bouchard, G (2010) Why do women do the lion's share of housework? A decade of research. Sex Roles 63(11–12): 767–780.

27. Thompson, L (1991) Family work: Women's Sense of Fairness. Journal of Family Issues 12(2): 181–196.

28. Keizer, R., Schenk, N. (2012). Becoming a parent and relationship satisfaction: A longitudinal dyadic

perspective. Journal of Marriage and Family, 74, 759-773.

29. *English Standard Version Bible*, 2016. ESV Online. https://www.biblegateway.com/passage/?search=Genesis+2%3A18&version=ESV

30. *English Standard Version Bible*, 2016. ESV Online. https://www.biblegateway.com/passage/?search=I+Corinthians+11%3A+11-12&version=ESV

31. *English Standard Version Bible*, 2016. ESV Online. https://www.biblegateway.com/passage/?search=Jeremiah+1%3A5&version=ESV

32. Leeder, E. (2004). The family in global perspective: A gendered journey. Thousand Oaks, CA: Sage Publications. 1-305.

33. Lucy A. Hawke (2007). Gender Roles within American Marriage: Are They Really Changing?

34. Bobby Akoi, (2015). Polynesian Men Do All the Cooking?

35. Bernard, J. (1981). The good-provider role: Its rise and fall. *American Psychologist, 36*(1), 1–12.

36. David, F. P. (1994). The Roles of Husbands and Wives in Household Decision-Making. *Philippine Sociological*

Review, *42*(1/4), 78–93.

37. Joshi, A., Kale, S., Chandel, S., & Pal, D. K. (2015). Likert scale: Explored and explained. *British Journal of Applied Science & Technology*, *7*(4), 396.
38. Institute of Behavioral Research. (2009). *Survey of Transformational Leadership* (TCU-STL-S) [Measurement instrument]. http://ibr.tcu.edu/wp-content/uploads/2013/06/tcom-STL-S-sg.pdf
39. Cech, E. A., & Rothwell, W. R. (2020). LGBT workplace inequality in the federal workforce: Intersectional processes, organizational contexts, and turnover considerations. *Ilr Review*, *73*(1), 25-60.
40. McCandless, S. (2022). # MeToo and human resources legislation: istory, legal patterns and prospects. In *Handbook on Gender and Public Administration*. Edward Elgar Publishing.
41. Storozhuk, S., & Hoyan, I. (2018). Gender equality in the context of social relations. *Bulletin of the Cherkasy Bohdan Khmelnytsky National University. Series Philosophy*, (1), 3-16.

42. Leite, T. H., Moraes, C. L. D., Marques, E. S., Caetano, R., Braga, J. U., & Reichenheim, M. E. (2019). Women economic empowerment via cash transfer and microcredit programs is enough to decrease intimate partner violence? Evidence from a systematic review. *Cadernos de Saude Publica*, *35*, e00174818.

About The Author

Dr. Femi Ogunjinmi is a global relationship expert, TV host of the Dr. Femi Show, which has been seen in over 60 million households on Roku TV, United Nations Representative, recipient of the World Civility Day National Relationship Expert Icon Award, and author of several books, including Revelations of Relationship, How to Tell If Someone Truly Loves You, and his two most recent books: Best Relationship Advice for Singles, Dating, and Marriage.

Dr. Femi has appeared on NBC, ABC, FOX NEWS, The New York Weekly, USA TODAY Magazine, and numerous other media outlets. He has appeared on major media platforms such as The Word Network, Radio One, and TEDx. His TEDx talk has over 5 million views and is growing by 100,000 views per month.

Dr. Femi runs his own relationship programs in addition to keynoting and speaking at conferences across the United States and abroad. His signature conference, "Revelations of Relationship Seminar," is held every year in the United States and has also been held in Nigeria. He also organizes retreats for men called "Becoming the Man She Wants" and for couples looking to improve their relationships called "Becoming the Person Your Partner Wants."

Dr. Femi is the founder of National Relationship Equity Day, an organization that has created a national awareness day that is celebrated every June 24th. National Relationship Equity Day is dedicated to eliminating gender inequity in relationships and promoting the use of gifts, values, skill sets, constraints, and interests as alternative ways of defining roles in relationships.

Dr. Femi earned a Ph.D. in Christian Counseling (Marriage, Family, and Child Therapy), a Master of Business Administration (MBA), a Bachelor of Science (BSC) in Biology, and a certificate in Financial Management as a scholar. United Graduate College and Seminary International has also conferred upon him an honorary doctorate of humanity. Dr. Femi's professional experience includes working as a senior cyber security analyst and consultant for top organizations such as the DoD, USAID, USDA, State Department, Harris Corporation, SAP, and Centurylink. He founded Improvement University, an online learning platform that teaches people professional and personal skills. In January 2020, Dr. Femi was inducted into the World Book of Greatness. He is married to Dr. Queen Victoria Ogunjinmi, whom he affectionately refers to as his all-inclusive wife, and they have two wonderful children.

Made in the USA
Middletown, DE
28 June 2023

33888686R00091